TOO NUMEROUS TO KILL

Jefferson slammed into the enemy line, striking out, killing enemy soldiers. He was screaming at the top of his lungs, swinging right and left. The enemy fell back under the surging charge. They jumped from the bunkers and ran across the open ground, some of them forgetting their weapons. Panic spread through them as they tried to get away from the screaming human soldiers.

Platt looked around at the destruction inside the camp, at the abandoned equipment and the bodies of the dead. He turned to Jefferson. "They going to attack again?"

Jefferson looked at the remains of his camp. "They'd be stupid not to."

Ace Books by Kevin Randle

Jefferson's War Series

THE GALACTIC SILVER STAR
THE PRICE OF COMMAND
THE LOST COLONY
THE JANUARY PLATOON
DEATH OF A REGIMENT

JEFFERSON'S WAR

DEATH OF A REGIMENT

KEVIN RANDLE

ACE BOOKS, NEW YORK

This book is an Ace original edition,
and has never been previously published.

DEATH OF A REGIMENT

An Ace Book / published by arrangement with
the author

PRINTING HISTORY
Ace edition / November 1991

ISBN: 0-441-38441-2

Ace Books are published by The Berkley Publishing Group,
200 Madison Avenue, New York, New York 10016.
The name "ACE" and the "A" logo
are trademarks belonging to Charter Communications, Inc.

PRINTED IN THE UNITED STATES OF AMERICA

10 9 8 7 6 5 4 3 2 1

PROLOGUE

ON BOARD THE SS *GEORGE PATTON*

CAPTAIN O'DELL SAT on the bridge and stared at the display screen, watching as the fourteen ships, ten military escort vessels and four science research craft, entered the star system. Escort duty was boring, even if they were at the edge of the explored universe. He had to take orders from the chief scientist, a mousey man who refused to listen to reason. If there was something to be learned, the scientist forced the ships into areas, systems, near stars, that O'Dell would prefer to avoid, but his orders were clear.

O'Dell kept his eyes on the screen, staring at the bright point at the bottom right. That was the sun of the system. He could see the disk of a single planet near the center of the screen but knew there were more.

"Something moving out there," said one of the officers.

O'Dell grunted and turned in his chair. "Please provide a little more information."

"Aye, sir. I have one, two, three objects coming from behind the star. Under power."

"Identity?"

"They have not answered the IFF, but then they're far enough away that they may not have received the signal yet."

"Put them on the screen," said O'Dell.

The image there shifted and then the star was in the center. "Still outside visual range," said the officer. "Sensors have picked them up."

O'Dell leaned forward as if to see better. The star's brightness masked any movement.

"What's their heading?" asked O'Dell.

"They aren't coming at us, sir. I don't think they know we're here."

Another of the officers said, "There's a spread of them. Now more than a dozen."

O'Dell tried to see them, but the screen, the sensors, refused to resolve the image. O'Dell felt sweat bead on his forehead and drip down his sides. Suddenly he was hot. He swiped at his face, his eyes locked on the screen.

"Anyone have any ID on them?"

"No, sir."

The communications officer turned. "I've a signal from the science vessel."

O'Dell shot him a nasty glance and then said, "Give me audio on it."

"Aye, sir."

"We wish to travel to the seventh planet now," said a voice that sounded as if it didn't have a care in the universe. "Please change course to intercept and then orbit."

O'Dell tore his eyes from the screen and looked at the commo officer. "You tell them negative."

"Aye, aye, sir." The Communications officer relayed the message.

"Captain O'Dell," said the scientist, "I might remind you that you are here to serve."

O'Dell, angered at the way the scientists used the radio, as if it were a telephone in their apartments or offices on Earth, touched a button. "Clear this frequency immediately."

"Captain . . ."

"Fry, you cut them, off, and you tell Captain Alverez to get the civilians away from the radio until we figure out who is coming at us."

"Aye, sir."

O'Dell had to stand up. He pushed himself out of his chair and took a step toward the screen. Again, he wiped the sweat from his face and wondered why engineering couldn't get the air conditioning to work better. It was too damned hot on the bridge. A man couldn't think when it was that hot.

"Twenty ships, Captain."

O'Dell looked at the officer sitting at the radar and sensor station. A young woman who was on her first interstellar cruise. She seemed to be very calm about it.

"Targeting," said O'Dell.

"Targeting, aye."

"We've a spread of unidentified ships out there. I want you to be aware of them."

"Aye, sir."

O'Dell turned back to the communications officer. "You get an IFF response?"

"Negative, Captain, they do not answer our interrogation, friend or foe."

"Captain, they've spotted us. Sensor scan against our hull. Strong burst of electromagnetic radiation."

"Captain, they've turned toward us and are spreading out."

O'Dell remembered his training in the simulator. One lesson was drilled into him. If a ship was coming at him, it was the enemy. Especially when there was no identification of that ship.

"Targeting, do you have them in your sights?"

"Targeting, aye."

O'Dell rubbed the side of his face. He felt as if he were in a steam bath and wrapped in warm, damp towels. His uniform was soaked.

"They've increased their speed, Captain."

"Still no response to our interrogation?"

"Negative, Captain."

Now they appeared on the screen. Small black dots coming out of the glare of the solar disc. He could see no detail on the ships.

O'Dell wanted to do something, but he didn't want to fire on what might be friendly aliens. As far as he knew, a state of war did not exist between Earth and any other planet. He didn't want to start one.

"They're firing," said a voice.

O'Dell saw the sudden sparkling on the sides of the enemy ships. It looked as if they were bursting into flames.

"Beam weapons and missile barrage."

"Screens up?" asked O'Dell.

"Up and steady."

"Thirty seconds to first contact."

"Captain, this is Targeting. We're ready."

O'Dell nodded, knowing that no one in Targeting could see it. "You are cleared to fire. Lasers and then missiles. Torpedoes to follow fifteen seconds later."

"Targeting, aye."

O'Dell kept his eyes on the screen. That was the only indication that they'd fired in response. There was no recoil from the laser and beam weapons and no sudden burst of sound from the missiles or torpedoes. Tiny points of light appeared on the screen, all of them aimed at the enemy ships.

"Targeting," said O'Dell. "Hit the incoming missiles."

"Targeting, aye."

Without turning, O'Dell said, "Communications, get me Captain Bartlet."

"Bartlet, here," said a voice.

"Escort the science vessels out of here," said O'Dell. "One-hundred-and-eighty-degree turn. You are cleared to make the run at top speed."

"Aye, sir. Wouldn't it be better for me to remain on station? The science vessels can retreat on their own."

"I don't want them left with no protection," said O'Dell. "You are free to maneuver at your descretion."

"Aye, sir."

The first of the enemy missiles was now in range. There was a sudden flash of bright light as it detonated far short of O'Dell's fleet. More lasers flashed and more of the enemy missiles vanished.

But the enemy responded, launching more missiles, a spread of more than a hundred of them. At the same time, the beamed weapons opened fire, dancing across the screens of O'Dell's fleet.

"Shields are heating," said a voice.

The enemy missiles began to corkscrew. Beams flashed out, missed, and the enemy weapons raced in, closer.

"Targeting," said O'Dell.

"They've changed the pattern," said Targeting. "We're compensating now."

Two more missiles exploded.

The beams continued to play across the fleet. An officer said, "Shields are superheating."

"Their fleet is beginning to fragment," said an officer. "Looks like they intend to pursue the science ships."

"Targeting?"

"Aye, sir, we monitored. We're tracking those ships now."

"Take them under fire."

A spread of torpedoes appeared suddenly, heading toward the enemy. A moment later each of the torpedoes detonated, the victims of the enemy beams.

"Targeting," said O'Dell, the first hint of nervousness in his voice.

"We're on it, Captain."

"Shields beginning to buckle, Captain. Damage to the bow compartments. Engines beginning to superheat."

O'Dell, his eyes focused on the enemy, wiped a hand over his chin. He turned and looked into the faces of the bridge crew. They were scared. They wanted to get out. No one had told them they would face an enemy whose ships outclassed theirs.

"Engineering. Reverse course one hundred eighty degrees. Begin a gradual acceleration."

"Engineering, aye."

"Communications, launch a drone with a record of what's happened here."

"Communications, aye."

O'Dell retreated and fell back into his chair. His eyes never left the enemy racing toward him. The enemy ships, now looking long and deadly, were twinkling, almost as if they were alive with fireworks. Bright flashes of color as beams, lasers and missiles were fired.

"Targeting, they're ripping us apart."

"Aye, sir. We're firing back."

But each time a spread of missiles was fired, or torpedoes were launched, the enemy destroyed them easily. Once or twice the enemy's missiles were destroyed in the fireballs, but the rest of the weapons ran true.

"Thirty seconds to impact."

"Engineering, let's accelerate," said O'Dell.

"Accelerating now."

"Impact in twenty seconds."

"Targeting?"

"We're aiming at the missiles."

Another of them exploded no more than a thousand kilometers from the ship. But that didn't bother the others. They still came on.

"Impact in ten seconds."

"All hands, brace for impact," said O'Dell. He gripped the arms of his chair, knowing that it would do nothing for him if the missiles hit a vulnerable spot.

There were two bright flashes as lasers ripped through the warheads of the missiles, detonating them early. The light washed over the ship, the radiation that would kill the unprotected, but O'Dell and the crew felt nothing.

"Shields still up."

"Engineering. We've minor damage. Aft shield is down. We diverted power to the forward shields."

And then the remainder of the enemy missiles hit. A few detonated against the shields, but the force of that energy was enough to tear them apart. Now the vessel rocked to the side. There was an explosion from somewhere deep in the ship.

O'Dell hit a button on the arm of his chair. "I want damage reports now."

"We've lost our main drive," said Engineering.

The acceleration ceased, but the speed didn't decrease. They had no power to maneuver without bleeding off the speed.

O'Dell slammed a hand onto the arm of his chair. "Targeting, I want you to salvo everything. A single target. Take out one of their ships."

"Targeting, aye."

O'Dell could hear the panic in the man's voice. He knew that it was a desperation move designed to kill one of the enemy. A desperation move designed so that they didn't die in vain.

Now the enemy seemed to lose interest in them. They began to attack the other warships. Missiles, beams, lasers were fired at them.

O'Dell said, "Communications, have everyone maneuver at will and for the safety of their ships."

"Aye, sir."

"Visual, show me the rest of the fleet."

The scene on the screen changed. Now it was focused on the ships of his fleet. Four small ships filled the screen. They were on line, firing at the enemy.

A moment later one of the ships began to glow dully as the shields were attacked by the enemy beams. It brightened, became brilliant and then the ship vanished. When the glow faded, there was an expanding cloud of debris.

"Jesus," said someone.

Now the enemy attacked a second ship, concentrating on it. Missiles and beams. It fought back, killing missiles in flashes of bright light. But there were too many of them. The ship was hit a dozen times. Explosions ripped through it. Fire burst from the rear and then the ship vanished.

"Engineering," said O'Dell. "We need to get out of here now."

"Sorry, Captain. We're working on it. Two hours minimum."

"Jerry, if we don't get out of here now, we're not going to make it."

On the screen, the last of the ships was beginning to accelerate, running toward the rear. The back half of it burst into fire, and the craft vanished in a flaming explosion.

"My God," wailed someone on the bridge.

"We don't have time for that right now," said O'Dell. "We've got to work to get ourselves out of this."

"Enemy formation is fragmenting," said the radar officer.

"Maybe we'll get out of this yet," said O'Dell. "Targeting, let's hold our fire for a moment."

"Aye, sir."

O'Dell sat quietly, watching the maneuvering of the enemy and listening to the sounds of the instruments on the bridge. Two officers were quietly discussing the reading. One of them finally turned.

"Captain, they're going after the science vessels."

"Helm, turn to intercept."

"We'll bleed off our speed, Captain."

"Make the turn," said O'Dell. "Engineering. How are you doing?"

"Main power in fifteen minutes, if we catch a couple of breaks."

"We need it now," said O'Dell. There was no response from Engineering.

"They're firing on the science vessels."

"Targeting, you are cleared to fire. Take the closest target under concentrated fire."

"We have only missiles and the lasers."

"Use everything you have, Targeting."

"Aye, sir."

An instant later the sky around them was bright with the tiny rocket engines of the missiles. They corkscrewed their way toward the closest enemy, diving and climbing and spinning as the ship tried to evade them. Beams from it flashed and some of the missiles detonated or were cut in half. But the rest continued on, homing on the enemy. An instant later there was a blinding flash that turned the screen into a blob of intense light. When it faded, the enemy ship was gone.

Cheering erupted on the bridge. O'Dell ignored it, knowing that it would be short lived. He'd used all his missiles to eliminate one of the enemy ships. There were more than a dozen left, and the laser weapons weren't having much of an effect on them.

"Science vessels have been destroyed," said a quiet voice, barely audible over the cheering.

O'Dell glanced at the officer and nodded as the cheering died quickly. The pale faces were staring at the flatscreen, watching as the battle began to end. O'Dell felt light headed and slightly sick, but ignored his feelings.

"Communications, I want a narrow-beam transmission, aimed at Earth. Two-second bursts, encoding everything that has happened to us."

"Earth won't receive it for forty years," said the communications officer.

"I didn't ask for a lesson in the speed of radio waves. Make the transmission."

"Aye, sir."

"And I want a spread of probes containing the same data launched, one aimed at each of our bases."

"Aye, sir."

"Shields are beginning to superheat again."

"Bridge. Engineering. We can maneuver."

"All right," said O'Dell. "Helm, make for the science vessels."

But as they turned, they could see that it was too late. The last of the science ships, along with the escort, blossomed and vanished. O'Dell and his ship were all alone. There was no one to help them.

"Engineering, give me full speed out of here."

"Aye, sir."

"Probes launched," said the communications officer.

For a moment O'Dell thought they were going to get away with it. The fleet was gone. There were clouds of debris falling into orbits around the star. There would be nights on some of the planets alive with meteors thanks to the junk that they had produced. That junk could also mask a single ship as it attempted to flee.

"Communications, Radar, Targeting, shut down all equipment. I want nothing transmitted."

"Aye, sir."

O'Dell hoped the enemy would think that his was a dead ship now on automatic control, fleeing the battlefield. He hoped they wouldn't waste their time or energy chasing him to finish him. He hoped to get clear so that he would live to fight another day.

The enemy fleet turned toward him. They too began to

accelerate, and in minutes it was obvious that O'Dell would not be able to outrun them. He could only hope they thought his ship was dead.

But then the range was under five thousand kilometers, and each of the enemy ships opened fire.

One officer had enough time to shout, "Shields are buckling. Hull is superheating."

And then the ship exploded in a flash that rivaled any that the battle had produced. The glowing cloud spread slowly, dimming as it did. The enemy had won the first battle.

1

ABOARD THE SS *CARL SPAATZ*

COLONEL DAVID STEVEN JEFFERSON had never attended a staff meeting where all twelve regimental commanders were present. Normally the duties of some of the officers kept them from reporting for the monthly meetings. The distances involved, the loss of time, was something that overweighed the necessity of each regimental commander attending. Besides, closed-circuit, data-linked transmission made it possible for them to attend, after a fashion. If nothing else, they could review everything that had transpired.

But not this time. The general had ordered each regimental commander to be there regardless of the time, effort and expenditure of energy required. This was a meeting that no one could miss.

As soon as Jefferson stepped onto the divisional flagship, he knew that something was up. The level of activity was higher than he'd ever seen it. Security regulations that had been unobserved for more than a year were being enforced. Radio transmissions, all forms of electromagnetic transmissions, sensor probes and sweeps, anything that produced a signal that could be detected, were carefully monitored. Survival suits that had hung in place without being inspected had been cleaned, recharged, and were again ready.

As he walked down the corridor with Lieutenant Colonel Rachel Davies, he said, "What in the hell is going on here?"

Davies was a tall, slender woman with jet-black hair cropped very short. Hers was a muscular build with broad shoulders. Her face was narrow, her chin pointed. A ragged scar ran from her right eye to the side of her mouth.

"General alert," she said.

"That I know," said Jefferson. "What I don't know is why. What's happened?"

They came to a hatch. It was closed and sealed. Another precaution. If one section of the ship was penetrated, the air would not escape from the other sections. It made travel through the ship slow and unhandy, but it also underscored the heightened alert status.

Davies shrugged. "I don't know. Just that I had to leave my regiment and take the fastest transport to get here. I don't like leaving my exec in command. He has some funny ideas about how a military unit should function and takes every opportunity to put those notions into effect."

"Which you overrule on your return," said Jefferson.

She laughed. A single bark. "Of course. It's my regiment and not his."

Jefferson touched the keypad next to the hatch, watched as it cycled and then slipped open automatically. "After you," he said.

"Full colonels first," she said.

Jefferson grinned and stepped through. He waited for Davies and then closed the hatch. There was a guard standing nearby, armed with both a pistol and rifle and wearing a wire mesh uniform of dark gray. Jefferson couldn't see the point of it because by the time the guard was into the fight it would be nearly over. If the enemy got that far, the ship was lost.

As they moved forward, toward the bow, there was even more activity. Men and women were running down the corridor carrying computer updates, orders of battle, operational plans and a dozen other things. They dodged around the senior officers, diving into cabins and offices. There was the clatter of printers, the whining of disk drives and the constant stroking of keyboards.

"Christ," said Jefferson.

"Maybe it looks worse than it is."

"You ever been on the flagship before?" asked Jefferson.

"Twice."

"You ever seen it like this?"

She shook her head. "No. Never like this. It was always a little laid back. Relaxed. The general let the regulations slide for the efficiency of the division."

"Yeah," agreed Jefferson.

They came to the main conference room. There were two guards at the entrance, both armed with rifles and pistols. Just their eyes were visible through the mesh of wires they wore. As Jefferson and Davies approached, one of them leaned over and touched the keypad to open the hatch.

"Thank you," said Davies.

"Yes, ma'am," the soldier responded.

They entered and found the majority of the other regimental commanders, the three brigade commanders and most of the general staff there already. Jefferson saw the chair reserved for him and took a step toward it. He stopped and said to Davies, "Dinner later?"

"Of course."

Jefferson nodded and moved to his chair. He sat down, looking at the colonels on either side of him. They commanded the Ninth Interplanetary Infantry and the Eleventh. Jefferson had the Tenth.

"Good to see you again, Mac," said Jefferson to Colonel Maxwell Taylor the sixth.

"Same," said Taylor. "I think."

The hatch opened again, and the last two regimental commanders entered. They took their seats, and the buzz of conversation increased.

"What the hell?" said Taylor, looking at Prescott, the Chief of Staff of the division.

"Full briefing as soon as the general gets here," said Prescott. "Until then . . . " He held his hands out, palms up, shrugging.

"This is unprecedented," said another of the commanders.

The senior brigade commander, a brigadier general named

Rivera, said, "Colonel, I would like to know what is happening, and I'd like to know right now." His voice was quiet but there was a hard edge to it.

Prescott turned to face the general and said, "I have my orders, sir."

Before anyone could speak, a hatch opened and the divisional commander stepped in. He glanced at the assembled officers. Prescott, looking relieved, said, "The commander."

The staff and commanders climbed to their feet. The general moved to the head of the table where there was a single high-backed chair. He pulled it around and then looked at Rivera and Prescott.

Sitting, the general said, "Be seated." Then to Rivera, he added, "I don't appreciate your attempts to countermand my instructions to my staff."

"Excuse me, General," said Rivera, "but I'm interested in the reasons for being summoned here."

"It is enough that you were ordered here."

"Yes, sir."

Jefferson examined the general. Jefferson knew the man was approaching sixty but he looked to be under forty. Tanned and fit with black hair that seemed to be darker than Davies', it looked a little too thick, as if it had had some help. His features were thin, without a sign of age.

"Ladies and gentlemen," said the general. "I have called you here for a specific reason. Never before in our travels through space have we encountered the threat that now faces us. It will take all our resources, all our courage, to end it."

The general touched a button recessed into the arm of his chair. Panels fell over the portholes that viewed into space. The conference room darkened, and a cloud of swirling gases appeared over the center of the long narrow conference table.

As the holo began to coalesce, the general said, "We first made contact with this race about nine months ago." He looked pointedly at Jefferson. "It was a skirmish with our side winning the victory. At that time, the enemy fled, and because we had recovered our people, we allowed them to go, running into space we have not explored."

"Good God," said Jefferson.

"That's right, Colonel. It was your regiment that made initial contact."

"We chased them away," said Jefferson.

"They're back," said the general. "More of them, and they're working their way toward Earth a system at a time."

The holo showed a formation of sleek, black ships. Needle-shaped, long and dark. Behind them was a second formation of cigar-shaped craft. Larger, gray-colored ships.

"Analysis of the formations and the tactics employed," said the general, "suggests that the lead craft are the battle craft. The ships behind are the troop carriers."

The enemy formation vanished, and the holo displayed a three-dimensional map of their section of the galaxy.

The general stood up and moved to the right. He stood behind the commander of the First Interplanetary Infantry Regiment. She was a small woman with short blond hair. Her left hand was missing two fingers, and there was a long scar on her neck. She seemed bothered by the general standing behind her. She shifted around, squirmed, but said nothing.

"We have decided to spread our division out, through these seven systems. They include a dozen inhabitable planets. Infantry is going to have to occupy the planets in the biospheres of the stars. Space-borne support ships, battle craft and fighters will be deployed to engage the enemy fleets as they move into each of the systems."

The holo changed slightly and began blinking with colored lights. An arrow appeared in the display and twisted around until it was pointing at a single planet.

"Given what we've seen of the enemy in the last two weeks, we believe that he is going to attack each of our outposts in turn, starting with the one here, in the Alpha Mensae. They've given no indication that they will bypass a system that contains a military force."

"Wait a minute," said Jefferson. "There is a single piece of information missing here. You're giving us intelligence about an enemy that we encountered once. You have not debriefed any of my regiment who came into contact with these beings. . . ."

"Colonel Jefferson. Debriefing your soldiers was unnecessary. When you took the planet, you also liberated a large number of humans. Our intelligence section has used them to put together a profile of our enemy. That was how we learned so much about them."

One of the other regimental commanders asked, "What does the enemy look like?"

The general touched his controls and the star systems vanished. They were replaced by a small creature, two feet tall, standing on the center of the table. It rotated slowly in the holographic display tank.

The creature was humanoid. It had a large head with no hair, large dark eyes, no ears or nose. The skin was gray and beaded, like the skin of a lizard. The arms and legs were skinny, not much thicker than bones. The hands had three long fingers and a stubby thumb. It was dressed in a silver jumpsuit.

"This is about half size," said the general.

"Hell,we can stomp the snot out of them," said one of the men.

"In a hand-to-hand fight," said the general, "we could probably crush them." He looked pointedly at Jefferson.

"We had only limited contact," said Jefferson. "They didn't have defenses against our lazer weapons, even though theirs were more powerful than ours, overloading the protective mesh quickly."

"There are modifications to the suits," said the general. "They can absorb more energy now."

"Tactics?" asked another man.

"Frontal assault," said Jefferson. "But they broke and ran when we didn't just roll over. No real understanding of military tactics."

"They understand them now," said the general. He touched a button and the image of the alien vanished. The lights brightened but the panels over the windows stayed down.

"They have been systematically attacking our outposts on their way through the galaxy. They seem to know where our home world is and are working their way to it."

"Jesus," said a woman.

"Ours, along with the Fourth Division and the Eighteenth Task Force, are being deployed."

Jefferson looked at the general. He then looked at the general staff. Older men and women. Soldiers who had been in space for fifteen years or more. Men and women who had worked their way up the ladder into the positions. Jefferson suddenly felt inadequate but suppressed the feeling. There were more important things to worry about at the moment.

"We have one week to get into position," said the general. "Fully deployed and ready for an attack, all along the main line of resistance."

"When do you think we'll be in contact?" asked another of the commanders.

"Those at Alpha Mensae will probably make contact first. That seems to be where they're heading."

"Why not concentrate the force there?" asked Rivera angrily.

The general looked at Rivera. "Because, General, if we fail to stop them, there will be no significant force between them and Earth. We are all that stand between them and the people of Earth."

"A delaying action?" asked Jefferson.

The general seemed to shrink in his chair. He shook his head but said, "A delaying action. We buy time with our regiments. Time until the full might of our military force can be recalled and deployed here."

Jefferson felt his heart sink as he stared at the general. He remembered the delaying actions that sprinkled history. Three hundred Spartans who were sacrificed until the rest of the Greeks could finish their festival. Just under two hundred Texans at the Alamo who died as Sam Houston tried to raise an army. And thousands of Americans at Corregidor, fighting alone for three months as the rest of the country tried to get onto a war footing. Delaying actions normally meant death for those fighting them.

"Formal assignments will be handed out in individual briefings." The general was quiet for a moment and then added, "I know that there are those of you who have hated the police actions we've been fighting. Those of you who wanted to fight in a real war have gotten your wish. I hope to hell that we're up to it. We cannot fail."

2

ABOARD THE SS *CARL SPAATZ*

THE OFFICER'S CLUB on the ship was something to behold. It was a huge area with a holographic display that covered one bulkhead and made it look as if it opened onto space. Sometimes, depending on the mood of the club officer, the holo showed scenes from great battles of the past. It was unnerving to be eating dinner as Confederate forces attacked Cemetery Ridge or as Patton's Third Army rolled through Nazi lines.

Jefferson sat at a table near the center of the club with Rachel Davies across from him, waiting for his dinner to arrive. It was surprisingly quiet in the club, but then it was surprisingly empty. Too much to be done for the majority of the officers to take the luxury of a long meal.

"I feel guilty about this," said Davies, her voice low.

"About what?"

"Being in here. We're practically alone. It seems that we should be doing something."

"In a couple of weeks we'll be on a planet's surface waiting to be attacked. Hot meals, air conditioning, luxury will all be gone. Do you think that the people here will deny themselves the luxury of the accommodations because we happen to be on the planet's surface?"

"No, but . . ."

"No, 'buts' about it. They'll be sitting here, eating the food, drinking the wine and looking out into space, and if they think about us at all, it'll be to say the same things that you're saying. In the end they'll eat the food and drink the wine and they'll forget all about us. Enjoy the fact that we have the opportunity while we have it."

"I know you're right, but I always feel left out if I'm not in the middle of the . . . in the middle of the action."

Jefferson grinned. "We all feel that way." He looked beyond her, at the holo display and studied the planets visible. One was a blue marble that could have been Earth, except there was no red planet or giant banded planet near it. It was obviously not the Solar System.

The food was brought by a waiter dressed in dark trousers and a white coat. He was a young man who looked as if he was badly scared. He set the food down in front of the two officers and then retreated immediately.

As soon as he was gone, Davies said, "I don't think I like the looks of that."

"What?"

"That man is scared. I think fear is sweeping the ship."

Jefferson looked down at the food in front of him. The mashed potatoes were running and the beans were cold. The steak looked as if it had been baked rather than broiled.

He sat back then and looked across the table. "Remember one thing," said Jefferson. "I've fought these creatures before. They weren't that formidable of a force. Their ships can be destroyed by our weapons. The advanced weapons."

"But they're on the attack now," said Davies. She picked up her fork, poked at her food, but didn't eat.

"Well, obviously," said Jefferson, "there is something that the general didn't tell us. We wouldn't be here if there wasn't something extraordinary. The point is simply that I've faced these creatures before, and I know the capabilities."

"I hope you're right."

Jefferson studied her carefully. The color of her skin was bad, as if she were about to be sick. Her hands were shaking. Quietly, he said, "We can take them."

"Don't you get scared before a battle?"

Jefferson didn't answer right away. Instead he thought of a green lieutenant crouching in the mud while a pillbox raked the ground around him. Flashing lightning gave the scene an unreal, unnatural quality. And then there was a sergeant, crawling out to destroy the pillbox while the lieutenant clutched the ground, trying desperately to disappear into it. Mason had destroyed the pillbox and Jefferson had won a medal for it.

"Yeah," he said. "I get scared. We all get scared, but we don't let it stop us."

"Until now," she said, "we've always had the upper hand in equipment. We were the ones who were farthest advanced. If we brought the whole of our military might to bear, we could destroy an opponent. Until now."

"And I'm saying that we are evenly matched." Jefferson grinned again. "One thing that hasn't been said, but was something that Torrence told me. Our enemy has not had to fight anyone for centuries. They are not a military-oriented race. That gives us the upper hand."

"I hope to hell that you're right," she said.

The briefing was held a little after nineteen hundred hours, in the small cabin to one side of the intelligence office. Only the intelligence officer, Lieutenant Colonel Karl Streeter, Davies and Jefferson were there. Streeter stood to one side, his arms folded across his chest.

"Colonel Jefferson, if I say anything here that is in conflict with your observations, please point it out."

"Of course," said Jefferson.

"Divisional headquarters," said Streeter, "has decided to deploy both the Seventh and the Tenth on the same planet, on opposite sides of it so that one or the other will be able to monitor all sections of space around you."

"Command?" asked Davies.

Streeter looked at her and shrugged. "You each retain command of your respective units."

"Overall command?" she said.

"Falls to the senior officer present," said Streeter. "Naturally."

She glared at him and then turned toward Jefferson.

Jefferson shrugged and said, "I don't see a situation where it would be necessary for me to take command of both regiments. Not with us separated by a planet."

"Sure," she said.

"If you have a problem with that," said Streeter, "I would suggest that you take it up with the general. I have an intelligence briefing to give here."

"Fine."

The lights dimmed and the holo tank brightened. He pointed at it and said, "This is Eighty-two Eridani some twenty light years from Earth. Alpha Mensae, where the first units will deploy is about thirty light years away, though it's not a straight line from Alpha Mensae to Eighty-two Eridani. It's felt, however, that the aliens . . . "

Jefferson interrupted. "I thought they were called Croatoans. That's what we'd learned earlier."

"Of course," said Streeter. "It's felt that the Croatoans will not bypass any heavily armed force, but will attack it to eliminate it before they begin the assault on Earth."

"Why?" asked Davies.

"Simply because it doesn't make good military sense to leave an armed force along your lines of communication. You eliminate it and proceed."

"It would seem to me," said Davies, "that you isolate it and then bypass it."

"That involves splitting your forces," said Jefferson. "Never split your forces in enemy territory without first learning the size and distribution of the enemy."

"We're talking about light years here," said Davies.

"With interstellar travel,with the Ryerson Drive, that makes no difference," said Streeter.

"Let's get on with it," said Jefferson.

"Eighty-two Eridani," said Streeter, "is a small system with seven planets, three dozen moons and the assorted debris found in all systems. There is a single gas giant which is one hell of a radio source and could mask our transmissions if conditions are not favorable."

"Great," said Jefferson.

The holo shifted to give them a view of the system. "The fourth planet is the one we're interested in." Again the view changed, focusing on the fourth planet. It revolved slowly, hovering over the table.

"Preliminary reports show a planet that is covered with lush vegetation, some animal life but no intelligent species."

"Why hasn't it been colonized?" asked Jefferson.

Streeter couldn't help himself. He grinned. "Temperature extremes from very hot near the equator to very cold at the poles and a lack of large supplies of water."

"Then how do the plants survive?" asked Davies.

"Who the hell cares?" asked Streeter. "This is not a botanical expedition."

"Water resources are important to us," said Jefferson.

"Of course they are, but we don't have to worry about where the plants get their water, do we?"

Jefferson stared at Streeter for a moment. Although Streeter was ten years older, Jefferson had the rank. He didn't have to listen to the sarcasm if he didn't want to.

"Just give us the information that we need," said Jefferson.

"Temperatures vary from forty degrees below zero at the poles to a maximum of fifty degrees Celius at the equator. There is a series of plateaus near the equator where it would seem that temperatures are less deadly. You'll want to look at those for the placement of your camps."

"You have files on all this?" asked Jefferson.

"Of course, both video and computer. Everything we know about the planet is now broken down for your use."

"Where'd you get the data?"

Streeter laughed. "Colonization office. They made a detailed survey of the planet but determined that it would cost too much to install colonists, not to mention that there was no guarantee that Earth crops could compete in that environment."

Jefferson stood up and moved closer to the holo display. The planet was revolving completely once every minute or so. A planet about the size of Mars.

Jefferson pointed at the plateaus. "There enough air there for us to breathe?"

"It'll be thin, but you can breathe it."

"What's being kept from us?" asked Davies. "The climate sucks, there isn't any standing water, and now you're telling us that the air is thin."

"In the last year, the star's temperature has fluctuated significantly. Solar radiation has increased and is approaching the danger zone."

"Good God. Why are we defending it?" asked Davies.

"Because it stands between the enemy and the Sun. It's that simple."

Jefferson stood studying the planet's surface. Only the largest of the physical features. The mountain ranges, the basins that might have held water once, canyons that might have been cut by rivers and the polar caps that extended down from the north and up from the south.

"You're sure that the air is breathable?" asked Jefferson.

"Yes."

Finally Jefferson sat down. He turned to look at Davies. "You have any questions?"

"When do they expect us to deploy?"

"You're to be on the planet's surface inside a week," said Streeter.

"Seems to bc a waste to me," she said. "You're assuming that these creatures . . . " She looked at Jefferson.

"Croatoans."

"These Croatoans will operate in the same fashion that we do. Can we make that assumption?"

"We can," said Streeter.

Jefferson was quiet for a moment, his eyes on the planet revolving above the table. An unextraordinary planet covered with thick green growth making it one of the few that he'd seen that had green vegetation. Trees, bushes, ferns—plants that might have evolved on Earth.

"Okay," said Jefferson. "What is everyone failing to tell us? There is something else going on here."

Streeter shrugged as if he didn't understand the question. He touched a button and the planet disappeared. Streeter sat down at the table, opposite both Davies and Jefferson.

"Contact has already been made," he said.

"I know that," said Jefferson. "I fought them once myself. So what?"

"No, other contact. A fleet out near the Zeti One Reticuli was attacked by them. They had time to make a distress call. Probe from the flagship."

"And the fleet?"

"Floating debris," said Streeter. He saw the look on Davies' face and added, "Not a front-line unit. Second string. An exploration outfit, but still an unprovoked attack."

"And now they're coming toward us," said Davies.

"Heading toward Earth," said Streeter. "We can't let them get near Earth."

"No," said Jefferson. "That we can't do."

3

FLAGSHIP OF THE TENTH INTERPLANETARY INFANTRY REGIMENT

IT HAD BEEN difficult finding accommodations for another infantry regiment. The ships had been designed and equipped for the transport of a single regiment. Each regiment had its own support ships along with the necessary vessels to insure their safety. Those of the Seventh had been taken and deployed elsewhere in support of another, make-shift regiment, leaving Jefferson's ships as the only means of transport for his regiment and for the Seventh.

Jefferson's staff hadn't been happy with the arrangements. Clemens, the flagship captain and the man who ran the naval portion of the operation, didn't like it. No one was happy. Systems were overtaxed, quarters that had seemed spacious were suddenly cramped, people had to spread sleeping bags on the decks for the shuttles, in offices that weren't used as often as others, in the wardroom and the galley and even in a few of the corridors. There were suddenly twice as many people but no more space for them.

Jefferson was now sharing his cabin with another officer. Torrence had been forced from her quarters so that Davies could have them. Torrence was bunking with the battalion commanders. Everyone was pushed into new areas.

Major Victoria Torrence, the regimental executive officer, visited Jefferson in his cabin. Jefferson chased Major Robert Montgomery out. Montgomery was a new man, having joined the regiment just before the call to division. He was a tall man, a thin man, with a nasty habit of talking to himself. Jefferson was sure that he would kill the man sometime in the next two weeks, regardless of his status with the division or his importance to the regiment.

Torrence looked at the gear stacked on most of the available floor space, at the boxes of computer files shoved up against the desk, and at the clothes that were laid out carefully on the floor.

"This is worse than down in the battalion areas," she said. She pushed some gear to one side and sat down on the cot. She was a tall woman, had long brown hair and was wearing a fatigue uniform that had been tailored to fit her perfectly. On long space flights there was little to occupy the troops. There were only so many exercises that could be run and only so much training that could be absorbed.

"I should have pulled rank," said Jefferson. He was leaning against the desk, his arms folded. He shook his head slowly. "Regimental commanders are not required to share their quarters with anyone."

"Wouldn't have looked good for the troops," said Torrence. "They're packed into every available space, but the commander still has his private cabin."

"I could have explained it so they wouldn't have minded," said Jefferson.

Torrence grinned. "A private with forty roommates isn't going to believe that the regimental commander needs a private cabin."

"No," said Jefferson, "I suppose not."

Torrence waved at the gear. "What's the story on this Montgomery anyway?"

"General assigned him to look at our operation. Some kind of liaison officer or efficiency expert who will see if we're fulfilling our charter."

"What the hell does that mean?"

"It means he's evaluating the combat skills of the regiment," said Jefferson.

"I would think that our last few operations would have demonstrated that."

"Paper-pushers never look for action, they look to see that all the squares have been properly filled, that all required training has been completed and that all the forms have been forwarded in their proper format. Operational abilities and combat efficiency aren't necessarily the prerequisites for a good regiment."

"Bull," said Torrence.

"I would agree," said Jefferson.

Torrence shifted uneasily, crossed her legs slowly and then said, "I'm not sure that having the Seventh here is a good idea. . . ."

"We had no say in that decision," Jefferson reminded her.

"Yes, sir, I understand that. I would like to isolate them more, if we can. Their training, discipline . . . ah, general appearance will have, has had a negative influence on our troops."

"You have any specifics?" asked Jefferson.

"I'd rather not say."

"Vicky, you know that I trust your judgment, but I can't make a informed decision without knowing what the hell you're talking about."

"I don't want to get any of our people in trouble."

"I'll pretend that I haven't heard a word of this, but I do have to know."

"There was an incident in the mess hall yesterday. Some shouting and pushing. One woman had to go to sick bay but that was because she tripped."

"Tripped or was pushed?" asked Jefferson.

"I think she really tripped."

"That all?"

"There have been some minor thefts. Little things disappearing, but I don't think it's really any worse than before the Seventh arrived. Of course now everyone is blaming them."

"Bad feelings growing," said Jefferson. "I'd better talk to Davies and see if we can think of something. We can't let this grow without doing something. Hell, we're all in the same army."

"But you have to be careful," said Torrence. "Wouldn't want to do anything to ruin the esprit de corps. That's hard to build but easy to destroy."

"Thank you, Major, but I do know something."

"Sorry," she said.

The computer on the desk bonged and Jefferson turned to hit a button on it. The screen cleared and the face of one of his NCOs appeared.

"Colonel, we've got a situation down in the shuttle bay. Need you there, sir."

"On my way." He turned off the computer and looked at Torrence.

"I don't know, sir."

Jefferson moved to the hatch. He opened it, let Torrence through and then closed it on the way out. They hurried to the mid-lift and took it to the shuttle deck. The door opened on a scene that irritated Jefferson. One side of the corridor had been stuffed with equipment. Boxes and piles and stacks of it. Access down the corridor was reduced, and if there were a sudden need to evacuate the ship by way of the shuttles, the men and women wouldn't be able to do it.

And it was dark in the corridor. Only half the lights were working and some of those were hidden by the gear. There were people sprawled everywhere, sitting on the deck or lying on it.

"We've got to clean this up," said Jefferson.

Torrence nodded, "Yes, sir."

They reached the shuttle bay and found the hatch open. It was supposed to be closed at all times in case there was a sudden problem with the doors or the hull in the shuttle bay. It was to protect the integrity of the ship. Jefferson shot a glance at Torrence who nodded her understanding.

They could hear the shouting from the shuttle deck. Jefferson stepped through and spotted a group of people standing in a tight circle. The crowd was shouting and pushing.

Torrence leaped forward, shoving her way through the knot

of soldiers. One or two looked as if they were going to strike her, but then saw who it was. They backed off.

As she shouldered her way to the center of the crowd, she shouted, "Attention. Everyone. Attention."

Slowly the shouting died away. The soldiers reluctantly came to attention. As they did, Jefferson made his way to the center of the circle.

One man was laid out, blood on his face, his skin a chalky white. Torrence was bent over him, examining him. Two others stood to the side, one of them had blood on the sleeve of his uniform.

"What happened here?" demanded Jefferson.

"Worthen tripped, sir. We were helping him."

Jefferson nodded and looked at the man with the bloody sleeve. "What happened."

"Like they said. Worthen tripped and hurt himself."

Jefferson shook his head. "You people know that I'm not going to let it go at that." He looked into the faces of the soldiers around him. There were times when the commander could look the other way and times when he couldn't. A little spirited inter-regimental rivalry was one thing, but it was beginning to get out of hand. Pushing and shoving were expected, but physical injury could not be tolerated.

Jefferson spotted one of his senior NCOs in the crowd. "Sergeant Jackson, I want you to get the people cleared out of here."

"Yes, sir."

Jefferson looked down at Torrence. She said, "He'll be all right. We'll take him to sick bay to make sure."

"Jackson, have a couple of people get Worthen to sick bay. And then I want to see you in my office."

"Yes, sir."

Jefferson knew that he could do no more there without making himself look bad. Besides, the soldiers weren't going to tell him a thing with fifty others standing around watching. Jefferson knew better than to try to force the issue there. He needed to separate the men and women and talk to them one at a time. It was the only way to learn anything useful.

He turned, let the soldiers move out of his way, and walked

toward the hatch. He didn't hurry. When he got there, he turned and saw that the soldiers were beginning to drift away. The trouble had been stopped for the moment.

The general sat in his conference room with his top staff officers. The holo showed a map of the section of the galaxy that contained the Earth and the area forty light years around it. Naturally, it was not to scalc.

There were red dots scattered on the fringes of the display. Toward the center, forming a semicircle with the Earth at the focus, were a number of bright blue dots. Those marked the locations of the regiments of the division as they were deploying.

"We should have our people in position within a week," said Prescott.

"Show me that," said the general.

The display changed slightly as the blue dots shifted to their final positions.

"There any indication of what the enemy will do?" asked the general.

Prescott shook his head. "They seem to be pulling together again." He stopped talking. "There are so many problems. We don't know where their home world is, but they seem to know ours. We don't know how many individuals they can field. We know nothing about them except that they had been traveling in space for longer than we have."

"Any further analysis of the destruction of O'Dell's command?"

"No, General. Nothing more there. We've analyzed the data from the probe but haven't learned anything new. We know our weapons are effective, but we need to equip our ships with more of them."

The general nodded and then waved. "Turn it off."

The holo display faded from sight. The lights came up slightly.

The general straightened himself and looked into the faces of each of his staff officers. "We have been less than honest with our commanders," he said. "We haven't told them everything we know."

"Jefferson has faced these beings before," said Prescott. "He did all right. He recaptured his missing soldiers and drove the enemy from their planet."

"He hit an outpost that was not prepared to face another space-faring race who understood military tactics. That would be like a line combat until hitting a company of National Guard soldiers. The National Guard is not ready for a military assault. They would be caught flatfooted and could do nothing other than retreat. But once they were clear of the fight, they would have valuable intelligence."

"Your feeling then," said Prescott, "is that we're about to face the front-line troops."

"Colonel," said the general, "I think O'Dell has faced them. They took him apart easily."

"He was able to destroy one of them," said Prescott.

"In a desperation move," said the general. "Now I don't have enough soldiers to face them, and I've got to divide my division to cover all the bets. I've got to sacrifice my people so that Earth can prepare."

"I don't think we're sacrificing the regiments," said Prescott.

The general felt the anger flare through him. A white-hot hate that burned out quickly. He was left feeling weak and sick. He turned and looked at Prescott and said, "That's exactly what we're doing. Making sure that the enemy must attack them, slowing their progress toward Earth. Our people are buying time with their lives. When this is over, we're not going to have much of a division left."

"I don't think it'll be that bad," said Prescott.

"I hope you're right," said the general, knowing that he wasn't.

4

FLAGSHIP OF THE TENTH INTERPLANETARY INFANTRY REGIMENT

LTC Rachel Davies did not wait for the camera to announce her presence. She burst into Jefferson's quarters, glanced at the major who was relaxing on his cot and then turned her attention to Jefferson who sat at the desk studying the computer screen.

"Just where in the hell do you get off ordering my people around?"

Jefferson ignored the initial outburst, finished typing and then turned away from the keyboard. With a quiet, controlled voice, he said, "If you have a problem, Colonel, I suggest that we discuss it alone."

She glanced at the major who was now sitting up. To him, she said, "Will you excuse us?"

For a moment it looked as if he was going to say something, but then he merely nodded. To Jefferson, he announced, "I'll be in the galley finding a cup of coffee." He stood and disappeared through the hatch.

The instant he was gone, Jefferson flared. "Don't you ever come in here like that again. You remember who is senior here, or I'll find a way of getting rid of you."

"Don't you give me that, Jefferson. The general hired me and only he can fire me."

Jefferson knew that was true, but he couldn't back down. Lowering his voice, he said, "Insubordination will not be tolerated. By anyone."

"I command my own regiment. You'd be well advised to remember that."

Now Jefferson grinned. "And I command this . . . light brigade," said Jefferson. "You'd be advised to remember that. Now, you have a problem, you sit down and we'll discuss it as two officers should."

She hesitated for a moment and then nodded. "Yes, sir."

When she was seated, Jefferson said, "The last thing that we can do is show any signs of a split between us. As the commanding officers, we have to be unified. They can't see us argue with one another. Now, if you have questions, tell me what they are."

Davies took a deep breath and said, "I'm sorry. I just don't want my people treated differently than yours."

"And I was presented with a situation that demanded some kind of positive action. I needed to end that problem and stop others from erupting. The easiest way was to get everyone out of there."

"Of course."

Jefferson stood up but didn't move closer. "Now, we do have a couple of problems coming at us. This overcrowding is wearing on everyone's nerves. Too many people and too little for them to do. I've got a food-service section that is overtaxed, as are some of the other support groups. . . ."

"Put some of my people on that," said Davies.

"I don't want combat troops reduced to KP," said Jefferson. "In one respect, I promote elitism. It's good for a military unit. If the combat troops feel superior to the support troops, I think that's fine."

"I try not to promote that in my regiment," said Davies.

"That's your privilege," said Jefferson. "But, I will not use combat troops to serve meals or clean latrines. Those who sit on the ships while the fighting goes on can do that. That's the price they pay for the luxury and the safety."

"Except when the ship is attacked."

"Then we all have the same problem," said Jefferson. "The

point is that the support troops will just have to work that much harder."

"Yes, sir," said Davies.

"Now, the question is, what are we going to do to keep our two regiments from fighting one another for the next week or so?"

"Training exercises?"

"We have limited . . ." Jefferson stopped and grinned. "Training exercises of a different nature. Your people pitted against mine. Closed-circuit broadcast. Maybe a little friendly wagering."

Davies nodded. "Of course. Make it into a sporting event."

"First thing," said Jefferson, "would be an obstacle course. Hell, we could spend two, three days running both regiments through, highest score wins. . . . Maybe some kind of special reward for those who shine during it."

"That would get their minds off everything else."

Jefferson returned to the desk and sat down at the computer keyboard. He thought for a moment and then asked for everything he could get on confidence and physical training. The screen blanked and then came back.

"You want to take a look at this?" asked Jefferson.

Davies stood up and moved closer, looking down over his shoulder.

"Easy as pie," he said. "We could have the navy put up the various obstacles in a matter of hours. Assign a value to them to be reduced the longer it takes."

"I'd like to add some targets to test skill with various weapons."

"Okay," said Jefferson. "That opens the door for some hand-to-hand competition. We could also add some tests for repairing equipment and setting up a base camp. We can get this going by tomorrow. Announce this in a couple of hours."

Davies nodded. "I like it. Make-work projects but something the troops can get into."

"Okay," said Jefferson. He stopped working and turned to look at her. "One thing. We have got to be united on this. You and I act as umpires and we settle disputes. You and I. No appeal and no grumbling."

"I understand," she said.

"I'll have my training officer meet with yours. We'll have to get Clemens to loan us some of his people too."

"Fine." She turned to go but stopped. "You understand, I have to protect my people."

"Certainly. That's the job of a commander. We just don't argue in front of the troops."

In the Alpha Mensae system, the Eighth Interplanetary Infantry Regiment watched as a battle took place in space over their heads. They didn't need any fancy instruments to watch. They could see their fleet engage the enemy, and the could listen to the battle on the direct-link radio. There were no secrets from the men on the ground.

It started as a fireworks display over them. Fiery displays as debris hit the night sky and rained down. The smallest of the debris, superheating during the plunge, blossomed into flame, leaving trails of red, orange and even green and blue.

"Don't worry about that," one of the officers had said. "It doesn't mean anything. Bullets dropped from there would begin to glow."

And even though the battle was taking place a hundred miles above the planet's surface, the soldiers on the ground could see the beams, the flashes of brilliance as missiles detonated, either against the hulls of ships or as they were destroyed by laser fire.

In the communications pod, the regimental commander, an old man named Delaney, listened to some of the inter-ship chatter. Listened to the orders as the fleet's captain tried to engage the enemy.

"McMasters, you are to accelerate to the right. Take that bastard there."

"I've got him."

"You're cleared to fire."

"Engaging."

"Landry, you're to disengage now. Retreat and hold in reserve."

"Landry, roger."

Delaney sat there, staring at the speaker, as if that would tell him what was going on. If the fleet stopped the enemy, then there would be no invasion. No battle on the planet's surface. That was what he hoped. Let the navy defeat the enemy and then land the shuttles to pick his soldiers up for transport out of there.

There was a sudden shout, and then a calm voice said, "Flag, this is Alzado. We're going in."

Delaney was surprised at the calmness in the voice. And then he wasn't. Soldiers were trained to take the extraordinary in stride. They were trained to sound calm on the radio because panic was contiguous. One shakey voice screaming into the radio could destroy a finely turned war machine.

Getting to his feet, Delaney moved out and looked up into the star-studded night. There was a pale flash and then a long, bright streak of flaming red. Delaney knew that it was something big. Lights danced behind it as the enemy pounded it to pieces. It fragmented and then exploded, a huge brilliant flash that faded slowly with thousands of meteors falling from it.

"Jesus," said a quiet voice, the awe unmistakeable.

"That's one," said someone else.

Delaney wanted to shout that a hundred men and women died to make that spectacular display, but knew his soldiers were aware of that. When you were waiting for the enemy to attack, the deaths of others took on a trivial nature. You were more concerned with your own survival. No time to worry about something you could do nothing about.

Delaney stood there and watched the death of the starship. He watched as the fiery debris reached the planet's surface. A moment later they heard the explosion of the ship. A distant rumbling that might have been thunder if they had been on Earth.

"Our guys aren't doing well," said the RTO.

Delaney nodded without speaking. Now his attention was fixed on the heavens above. It was difficult to follow the battle up there. Just lights in the sky. Flashes of brightness and the occasional rumbling if something exploded low enough.

"You think they'll get through?"

Delaney turned and saw Richardson, one of his battalion

commanders. A young woman who hadn't been with the regiment very long. A good soldier who now seemed to be more than a little frightened.

"I'm afraid so. Our fleet isn't designed for a major space battle. They're designed to repel small attacks and provide us with support."

"Seems like poor planning," she said.

"We've never run into a militaristic space-faring race before. I would imagine that things will change now," Delaney said.

"But not quick enough for us."

"No," said Delaney. He ducked back into the communications pod. To the RTO he said, "Can you put me in contact with the fleet captain?"

"He's pretty busy."

"Just make contact."

"Yes, sir." The RTO touched a couple of buttons and then leaned forward toward his console. "Batwing Six, this is Grounder Six."

"Go."

"Captain. Please maneuver for the safety of your fleet. Continued sacrifice will be pointless."

"Roger, Six. I believe that it's too late for that. They've got us hemmed in. Good luck to you."

"Thank you, Captain." Delaney looked at the RTO. "That's a brave man."

"Yes, sir."

Delaney ducked and stepped back outside. The aerial show was still being played out. There were more debris in the air now. Constant streaks of fire as the fleet was literally shot to pieces.

Delaney spotted one of his officers. "You'd better get the regiment ready to repel a ground assault."

"I take it that the fleet has failed."

"I think we can make that assumption."

"Yes, sir."

Delaney stood for a moment, his eyes on the skies. He was watching the death of the fleet and knew that his turn was coming soon. Now there wasn't as much of a show. Only a few bits of debris burning. And then there was another brilliant flare of light. A bright, glowing, expanding ball of fire that marked the death of another ship.

He turned away and looked at his regiment. It seemed so fragile now. Not enough people to stop the enemy. They didn't have the equipment, the weapons, the strength to do anything but die. He took a deep breath and felt tears fill his eyes. He didn't want his regiment to die. That was the last thing he wanted. But there was nothing he could do about it now. It was too late for everything.

5

FLAGSHIP OF THE TENTH INTERPLANETARY INFANTRY REGIMENT

THERE WERE FIVE judges in the umpire's shack on the simulator deck. Two from the Tenth, two from the Seventh and one ship's officer who was supposed to be neutral and who was supposed to break ties, if there were any.

Torrence, working closely with the exec of the Seventh, with the training officers, and the ship's historian, had put together a series of contests that were based on the old Combat Proficiency Tests given to members of the United States Army in the late twentieth century. They were designed to test the skill, ability, agility, and capability of the individual soldier. They tasked the strength, endurance, and intelligence of the soldier. Torrence and her group had modified them so that they would work on the simulator deck.

Jefferson and Davies stood behind the judges, looking at the monitors showing the first of the companies preparing for the tests.

Torrence pointed and said, "Each of the events is given a rating of one hundred points. Max all the events and you have six hundred points. Scores for each company will be averaged, and then the scores added and divided by the number of companies in a battalion. We'll have an overall rating of somewhere between five and six hundred after everyone is tested."

"Good," said Jefferson. "Who grades the companies?"

"That was a little difficult," said Torrence. "We figured that company officers would give the breaks to their people. We thought about letting that go, figuring everyone would do it and it would average out but didn't really like that plan. So, we decided that Colonel Davies's officers would grade our companies and we'd grade hers. Everyone would try to be fair that way. We, of course, will settle all disputes."

"Let's get it going then," said Jefferson.

Torrence shook her head. "Not so fast, Colonel." She grinned broadly. "The way we had it originally set up, only one battalion for each regiment could participate at once. That left the majority of the soldiers out to get into trouble." She touched one of the flatscreens. "There is a second competition going on using laser training rifles. Accuracy first and then a combat shoot with pop-up targets. That takes care of one more battalion."

"Very good," said Jefferson.

"Then, in the shuttle bays, where we've got the space, we've set up a competition on getting a working base camp established. Radios, tents and perimeter, all on a reduced scale."

"Three battalions," said Davies.

"Yes, ma'am," said Torrence. "And Captain Clemens has set up the conference rooms, the squad bays, the mess halls, and a number of other locations so that those not actively involved at the moment can watch the competitions. Everyone is now occupied."

Jefferson nodded slowly, slightly awed. "You put this together in twelve hours?"

"Yes, sir. I did, with the help of the others you see here. Colonel Davies's people were a big help too."

"Take a couple of medals out of petty cash," said Jefferson. He then touched her shoulder. "Seriously. I'm impressed with this."

"My job," said Torrence, "is the smooth running of the regiment. This will make sure that everything runs smoothly."

"I don't suppose," said Davies, "that I need to remind you that we have to be honest in our evaluations. The troops detect the slightest tone of favorism and we'll have more trouble than before."

"No, ma'am," said Torrence. "We all understand the importance of this."

"Good."

"Then the only thing left is to get started," said Jefferson.

"We'd hoped that you and Colonel Davies would make an opening announcement."

"I hadn't planned on that," said Jefferson.

"Just something about competitiveness between the regiments is a good thing as long as it's channeled in constructive avenues. Fighting between us does no good, but these contests will show everyone what we can do. Something like that."

"A joint statement," said Jefferson.

"Of course," said Davies.

"Closed-circuit through the ship," said Torrence. "Let everyone see it. Closed-circuit through the fleet."

"Certainly," said Jefferson. "Give me a moment."

"Troops are waiting," said Torrence.

Jefferson closed his eyes, his lips moved for a moment and then he was ready. He opened his eyes and nodded.

"Got a camera crew just outside, sir. Have them standing by in case we need to make a ruling."

Jefferson left the umpire's shack and saw a group of people standing in a clearing. Most of the simulator deck was set for jungle-warfare training. Hot and humid with thick, artificial vegetation. The center had been cleared for the obstacle course and the combat proficiency area.

He walked toward the clearing and said, "Whenever you're ready."

"Yes, sir." The crew scrambled around, getting the lighting set and then aiming the camera.

Steven Garvey, the lone civilian on the ship was there too, holding his own video camera. Garvey was a journalist assigned to cover the exploits of the Tenth. Jefferson didn't like him, didn't like journalists in general, but had to admit that Garvey had been fair with him so far.

"Mister Garvey," said Jefferson.

"Colonel." Garvey aimed his camera and asked, "What's the purpose of these games? Isn't it a waste of the taxpayer's money?"

"Leave it to you to think you've found corruption. No, these are actually training exercises. The troops are being tested on their proficiency in a wide range of events that are all directly tied to combat skills. By making it a competition rather than an annual inspection, we've created a healthy atmosphere and a real desire by the troops to do well."

Garvey shrugged. "Don't want the taxpayers to get the short end of the stick."

"Garvey," said Jefferson, "you don't care what happens to the taxpayers. You're interested in a story, pure and simple."

Garvey shrugged but kept his camera rolling.

Jefferson faced the other camera, the one run by members of the naval staff.

"Any time you're ready, Colonel," said one of the petty officers.

"Go." He waited until one of the men pointed at him. Then, smiling self-consciously, he said, "Ladies and gentlemen, welcome to the first contest between members of two separate regiments. The purpose here is additional training but against the backdrop of spirited competition."

He stopped, thinking that it sounded good but not sure that it meant anything. A lot of fancy words that sounded like double talk.

"Anyway," he said. "This . . . these, ah, games, will help us evaluate the readiness of each regiment to enter combat. And it'll give us something to think about as we head toward our next assignment."

He couldn't think of anything else to say and knew that the soldiers didn't want to hear the officers talk anyway. They wanted to get on with it.

Turning, he said, "Colonel Davies."

Davies moved forward, and the cameras focused on her. "I would like to agree with everything that Colonel Jefferson said. This will also give us a measure of the training levels in each regiment. But now I think it's time to begin. Good luck to everyone."

Jefferson half expected to hear a cheer, but there was none. No one around to cheer. Just the make-believe jungle and a few men and women operating the cameras.

As soon as the petty officer announced they were clear, Jefferson said, "Let's watch the preliminaries from the umpire's shack."

Garvey said, "Mind if I tape these games?"

"No," said Jefferson. "Have at it."

"Thanks."

Together Jefferson and Davies walked toward the umpire's shack. As they approached it, she asked, "You think this will work?"

"Hasn't been a fight since we announced the games last night. That's a good sign."

"Yeah, I suppose it is."

Corporal Thomas Forest stood at the starting line for the mile run. Forest was a small man with long legs, a barrel chest and thin arms. He looked as if he'd been bred for speed, and he was looking forward to the run. In training he'd always outdistanced his fellows. Once he got moving, once he got into the rhythm of running, his long strides ate up the distance. And finally, for the first time since he'd joined the infantry, that talent was going to be useful. Finally it would be necessary for him to use his speed.

Forest stood at the line with fifty other soldiers from the two regiments. Theirs was the second heat of the day. If he ran the mile under six minutes, while in uniform, while wearing combat boots, he would earn the maximum one hundred points. And if he turned in the fastest time, he would earn a bonus of fifty points for the company. That was his goal. Because there was no doubt he'd earn the hundred.

An officer from the Seventh was the starter. She was a tall woman with long hair and an angular face. Forest had noticed her eyeing him, but he ignored her as best he could. He wanted no distractions. He wanted to concentrate on the race.

She lifted a pistol and said, "On your mark. Get set. GO!" She pulled the trigger.

Forest leaped forward as if jabbed in the back with a sharp stick. He fell into his stride immediately, sucking at the humid air. Sweat beaded in seconds but he ignored that. He felt good. He felt that he could run forever.

Forest didn't pace himself. He glanced over his shoulder once and saw the pack falling farther behind. One man from the Seventh tried to catch up and then just stay with him, but Forest felt he had the strength of a dozen runners. He didn't need to worry about running out of steam. He could run forever.

On his second lap, he began to catch the slowest of the runners. He blew by them like they were standing still. He leaped around them, yelled "Track!" at them, but none of them understood the command. Forest didn't care. He was going for the record. Going for the gold, though he didn't understand what that meant.

It took him almost five minutes to run the mile. Five minutes of glory. And then he crossed the finish line and coasted to a stop. He walked on, barely breathing hard. The sweat dripped, staining his fatigue shirt, but it didn't matter. Forest had completed the run faster than anyone in either regiment. He had gained his moment of glory.

Sergeant Susan Arnheeter crouched in the throwing pit with the five dud hand grenades. The test was not of strength or speed but of accuracy. Those with the weaker arms weren't hampered by that. The trick was to hit the inner ring seventy-five feet away. Twenty points for each of them in the inner ring for a possible one hundred points. Skill was the key.

Arnheeter stood, her left side toward the pit, a grenade in her hand. She waited until the scorers were all in position and then for the judge to start the competition. Concentration was the key. Skill and concentration.

She kept her eye on the center of the pit and waited until the judge yelled, "You may begin."

Arnheeter cocked her arm, pumped once and then threw.

The grenade hit in the center and bounced. Twenty points. She grinned at that.

She worked her way through the grenades, throwing them with a fluid motion like a good center fielder trying to hit the cut-off man. Concentration and skill. She heard the words over and over as she threw her grenades. And when it was over, she scored her hundred points.

Sergeant Sarah Jane Williams stood in front of the dodge, run and jump course. There were paths through it. There were obstacles erected in the way. The soldier had to run for the obstacles, dodge around them and keep going. There was a ditch filled with a gooey mud. There was a short wall to leap and then a pivot point so that the soldier had to run back through it. Three more times. Four trips against the clock.

Speed wasn't the key to the race. It was agility. Dodging around the obstacles and not falling there or into the ditch. Run around them, leap over them and don't slip. That would give her the best time.

Williams stood at the starting line staring at the path she would follow. She wiped her hands on her chest to dry them. She took deep breaths trying to oxygenate her blood. She glanced right and left at her competition and then ignored them. They weren't important.

She heard someone count down and heard the shot. She ran forward, dodged to the right, around the first obstacle, took two running steps, leaped the ditch, and hit the next obstacle. She dodged left, clipped her hip and felt pain flash. She ignored it, leaped the wall and ran to the pivot point. She dodged around it, slipped slightly and then was running back through the course.

This time she made it with no missteps though the man running beside her slipped on the bank of the ditch. He twisted around but fell into it with a splash. He scrambled at the opposite bank but kept slipping. Williams ignored that as she ran, dodging and jumping.

As she ran through the course the final time, she saw one of the men of the Seventh was in front of her slightly. A step, maybe two. She wasn't going to let him win. She was not going to let her regiment down. As she rounded the last of the obstacles, she took a running step and dove for the finish line, her hand crossing it before the man from the Seventh.

Standing, she dusted herself off and grinned at the official scorer. "Put the Tenth down for a win."

Private Bruce Platt liked the low crawl, or the alligator crawl as the scorer called it. To do it, Platt had to throw himself to his belly and then using his hands and feet, propel himself along the ground as fast as he could. It tested the strength and the endurance. It wasn't an easy way to move the human body.

He stood on line with a dozen other men. A line of women stood behind him. They would run the next heat. On this one, the soldiers were segregated by sex.

When it was his turn, Platt moved to the line and crouched, then lay down flat. He brought one foot up so that he could push off and waited. The judge made sure that each contestant was behind the line. Satisfied that no one had a fraction of an inch advantage, she fired her starter pistol.

Platt sprinted out, shoving himself forward as fast as he could move. The resistance of the mat seemed to be higher than he remembered. The distance to the other end seemed to be farther than he remembered. Halfway down his arms began to ache. Halfway down the muscles of his thighs seemed to knot. Air burned his throat as he grabbed at the mat, rushing for the other end.

He hit the pivot point, spun and began the sprint for the finish line. He was the first to the pivot but he was running out of steam. It was harder than he remembered. It took more of his energy than he remembered.

At the halfway point he thought his muscles were going to give out. Pain radiated from his arms, his legs and invaded his chest. He couldn't get enough air, and a curtain of bright red was descending.

But in the back of his mind he could hear someone telling him to hurry. That the Seventh would win if he didn't hurry. There was cheering from those waiting for the next heats and those who had gone on in front of him. He could hear them, their voices sounding distant, as if they were in another part of the ship yelling.

He could feel himself slowing and knew there was nothing he could do about it. It was taking too much of his strength. Sucking it out of him. It was almost impossible to make himself move. The others would be catching him.

Ignoring the pain, Platt continued to pull himself toward the finish line. Vaguely, he was aware of the others around him. Of the other contestants trying to catch him. Now he was lightheaded, unable to concentrate. His strength was nearly gone.

But the end was in sight. He made the effort, stretched, and touched the finish line in front of the others. Then he collapsed, his head on the mat so that he could smell the overpowering odor of the rubber. It seemed to wrap his head in a fog so that he could taste it. Sweat poured from his body, soaking his uniform and pooling on the mat.

One of the women crouched near him and said, "Christ, it's only a game. No use killing yourself."

He twisted around and looked up at her. "I won, didn't I?"

"Yeah. You won."

"Then that's all that matters."

The first time that Corporal Cindy Hudson had used the overhead bars, she'd ripped her hands to pieces. They had been a bloody mess of torn flesh and open blisters. That had been the first time. No one had warned her about the damage she could do to her hands.

Now, after two years in the military, her hands had toughened up but not nearly enough. She wore gloves. There were those who said they couldn't get a proper grip with gloves and those who said that it slowed them down, but Hudson didn't care. She still remembered the pain as a lieutenant had poured a disinfectant on her hands. A burning that threatened to turn the lights out for a moment. Gloves solved the problem.

Hudson stood on the top rung of the ladder that led up to the bars. She waited until the judge said to get ready. She grabbed the first bar and hung by her hands, waiting.

"GO!"

Hudson began to work her way across the bars, reached the other side and turned for the run back. It was not a contest of speed. Hudson had to hit a hundred bars. That was it. Just make it across all one hundred at her own pace.

She reached the starting point and turned. It was only five trips across. A simple task. One that she'd done dozens of times in training. It stretched muscles, tightened the grip and strengthened her arms and back. Up and back a couple of times.

Again she reached the far end, turned and started back again. She'd done over sixty bars and was heading toward seventy-five. It was so easy that it was almost frightening.

And then she missed the bar. Swung at it. Touched it with her fingers and let it slip away. Missing it wasn't that much of a problem, but Hudson wasn't ready for the sudden strain on her other arm or her back. She twisted around, the pressure on her wrist increasing. She tried to hold on, but couldn't do it. She had to let go or break her wrist. She dropped to the ground and sank to one knee.

"Damn."

"Seventy-two," said the scorer.

"You okay?" asked one of the others.

Hudson stood up and ripped the glove from her hand. "Fine," she said. "Just fine."

In the umpire's shack, Torrence and the others watched the contests on a variety of flatscreens. They could keep track of all the contests and the running scores as the judges radioed the results.

Jefferson and Davies sat behind them, watching the progress. There had been no fights although there had been one shoving match when two runners had collided and both had fallen. The judge had declared that the member of the Seventh had tripped, inadvertently, the runner from the Tenth. The Seventh runner was disqualified, and the soldier from the Tenth would be allowed to run a new race. The decision seemed a little harsh, but the judge was from the Seventh, and Jefferson wasn't going to overrule the decision.

Davies leaned close and said, "It seems to be going well. Tension has bled off."

"Yeah," said Jefferson. "Healthy competition."

"Major Torrence, do you have any preliminary results?"

"From the Combat Proficiency Tests, it looks as if the Tenth holds a slight edge, but it's very slight. In the shooting contests, the Seventh holds the edge. And in the other contests, it's about a dead heat."

Jefferson nodded, wishing that his soldiers were winning in the shooting contests too. He wanted an all-around victory. But then, if they stayed close, it was probably for the best. Let each regiment capture a couple of the contests.

Glancing at the chronometer in the center of the console, Jefferson said, "Getting late in the day."

"I'd thought we'd let the companies finish the competitions they're in now and then call it a day," said Torrence.

"Good." Jefferson stood. "Colonel Davies, how about we catch some dinner and then check with intelligence?"

"Okay, Colonel," she said. "I suppose we have to make sure the war is still on."

"Major Torrence," said Jefferson formally, "we'll be in the wardroom and then in intelligence if you should need us."

"Yes, sir."

Together Jefferson and Davies walked out of the umpire's shack. As they reached the mid-lift, Davies asked, "What's wrong with your exec?"

"Wrong?"

"Seemed a little short there."

Jefferson shrugged. "She, along with the regimental staff, has put in some very long hours getting this competition put together. I guess she's tired."

"If you say so," said Davies.

Jefferson didn't understand but responded, "I say so."

6

FLAGSHIP OF THE TENTH INTERPLANETARY INFANTRY REGIMENT

CAPTAIN MICHAEL CARTER sat at his console in the intelligence office and tried to digest the data that was being sent to him. The office was small, with a big screen on the bulkhead, surrounded by a number of smaller screens. Two technicians were there with him, working on analyzing and cataloging the incoming data.

Jefferson, with Davies in tow, entered the office but didn't say a word. They waited until Carter was finished and had stood up, stretching with his fists pushing into the small of his back.

When he turned, Jefferson saw the look on his face. "What in the hell happened?"

"Lost contact with the Eighth Infantry a few hours ago," he said.

"That's nothing to worry about," said Jefferson. "Space is a big place."

"They were in the Alpha Mensae system and were required to launch probes on a regular schedule."

Jefferson felt a butterfly spread its wings in his belly. The beginnings of fear that things were beginning to race forward. To race at him.

"Probes malfunction all the times," said Davies.

"Yes, ma'am," said Carter. "But they've missed a couple of checks. One probe maybe but surely not two in a row."

"Anyone checking on it?" asked Jefferson.

"Nothing we can do from here," said Carter. "We've got to sit here and wait to see."

Jefferson turned to look at Davies, sure that she understood the implications of what Carter was saying. She'd been to the staff meeting, and she'd heard the general assign the Eighth to the Alpha Mensae system. That was the first area the enemy would attack if the enemy was coming. It was the picket system, and the 7th was the unit that would alert the rest of the division.

"Alpha Mensae isn't that far from us," said Davies.

"No. Couple of weeks, depending," said Jefferson. "They would have a couple of weeks to prepare, unless the enemy decided to hit them immediately. If they come on straight, the enemy could beat them to Eighty-two Eridani. If they wanted to eliminate everyone before the assault on Earth."

Jefferson tried to remember the star chart he'd seen earlier. Alpha Mensae and Eighty-two Eridani were not on a straight line to Earth. But the enemy, if he was trying to eliminate all forces before the assault, might attack anyway. No way to know.

Carter was still staring up at the big screen. He said, "For the moment, we don't have any answers."

Jefferson moved forward and slipped into one of the molded plastic chairs. He leaned forward, elbows on the console in front of him.

"The Eighth could have been destroyed, and we're playing games."

"Our turn will come," said Davies. "If the enemy is out there, our turn will come."

Jefferson wiped a hand across his face, surprised to find perspiration there. He didn't know what he was feeling. Betrayal of the Eighth, though there was nothing he could do for it. His mission was not to cover the Eighth's flanks, but to establish a base. A target for the enemy. A diversion so that the enemy wouldn't head directly to the Earth.

To Davies, Jefferson said, "I think we'd better meet with Captain Clemens. The sooner we can get into position, the better we're going to be."

"A rapid acceleration is going to end the games," she said.

"But it'll keep the soldiers occupied. Can't cause trouble when you weigh two or three times what you should. All you can do is lay there and wish that the acceleration would stop immediately."

"Is that going to help?" asked Davies.

"Who knows how valuable a couple of extra days on the planet's surface will be, but I think we've got to stop playing games and begin earning our pay."

Carter said, "Sir, I don't want you to make a snap decision here. There are a couple of things that might have caused the Eighth to fail to launch the probes. Division is making a run to find out what is happening there now."

"I think that we have to assume the worst," said Jefferson. "It's the only intelligent thing we can do."

Delaney and the men and women of the Eighth Interplanetary Infantry Regiment had expected aerial bombardment and then a ground assault. They had expected it to begin the instant that the fleet had been swept from the sky. But once the aerial battle was over, the enemy seemed to withdraw. Delaney decided it must mean that a space-faring race was not concerned with an army whose transportation was gone.

He'd watched the sun come up and had then moved along the defensive perimeter established by his regiment. They had some surface-to-space missiles, they had some heavy weapons that could engage the enemy at more than thirty or forty miles, and they had a light point-defense system that should inhibit the enemy. They were ready for anything except the lack of enemy action.

Delaney had spent the night haunting the communications pod and then the tracking center, searching for signs that his fleet had been victorious or signs that the enemy was coming. Overhead, space was clear. No one there.

Radio transmissions, both tight-beam and general broadcast, met with silence. His fleet was not answering, but that didn't mean complete disaster. It only meant they weren't answering.

Delaney was sure that the enemy would either come right at dawn, using the sun to mask the assault, or they'd come at night, using the darkness to hide it. Once they were through the night and the sun was up, he was sure that they were safe for another day. The enemy wouldn't appear until the next night.

To his executive officer, he said, "We go to a quarter alert, rotating every two hours. Those not on duty are free to sleep or eat or whatever. I want everyone rested."

"Yes, sir."

With the orders relayed along the line, Delaney walked back to the communications pod. The radios were filled with the normal pops and buzzes and chirps of static. There were no messages there. Only the semi-silence that marked the end of linked communications with the rest of the human race.

"Have you launched any of the communications probes?" Delaney asked the technician.

"No, sir," she said.

He looked at her. Like everyone in the regiment, she was wearing a mesh uniform designed to absorb the energy of beamed and laser weapons and to disperse it, using some of it to recharge the battery packs worn at the belt. But she'd stripped off the hood that left only the eyes uncovered. It was lying on the console near her fingers. She had short blond hair that stuck out at all angles, the result of pulling the hood free.

"Launch a communications probe," he said. "General direction of Earth. It is to broadcast nothing until it is three light years from here. Then standard radio transmissions."

"Yes, sir." She hesitated, her fingers over the keyboard. She turned and looked up at him. "Are they going to come after us?"

"I would have thought they'd have landed already. Maybe they're going to bypass us because we have no ships."

"I hope so." She bent back to her work.

Delaney left the communications pod and realized that he felt the same way she did. He hoped the enemy had left the system because he knew there was no way they could withstand an assault. The enemy now controled the space overhead. He could drop bombs, use lasers, or land an assault force and there was nothing that Delaney could do about it. His response options were limited now that his fleet was gone.

The executive officer, Sharon Mony, approached. She was a short woman who had seen action during three different campaigns. Like most combat veterans, she was not anxious to see it again. She had proven herself before and felt no need to prove herself again.

"I've got about half the regiment eating a cold breakfast now. A quarter on alert and a quarter trying to catch some sleep. I don't think many of them will be able to sleep. Not after what they saw last night."

"I thought they believed it was fireworks," said Delaney.

"I think they all know what it meant. They were being brave so the others wouldn't leap in their shit. I think they're all getting scared."

"So am I," said Delaney.

"It's the waiting," said Mony. "Gives you time to think. Once the fighting starts, you're too busy to think and too busy to be scared."

There was a sudden blast overhead and both Delaney and Mony ducked in reflex. Delaney straightened first and laughed. "Sonic boom."

"I think they'll be coming now," said Mony. She turned to run back along the line.

Delaney looked up, hoping that the ship that had created the sonic boom was one of theirs, but he could see nothing other than a thin white line in the bright blue of the sky. That was the vapor trail of the craft. No way to identify it.

The technician from the communications pod appeared. Her face was white with fear. "Message for you, sir. They've asked for our surrender."

Delaney took a deep breath and walked toward the pod. He let the technician fall in beside him. Just to make conversation, he asked, "What's your name?"

"Soter, sir. Linda Soter."

"Haven't been with us long, have you?" said Delaney.

"No, sir."

"I try to meet all the new people as they're assigned to the regiment."

"I was . . . I replaced one of yours who got sick just before deployment."

"Bet you're not happy about that now," said Delaney.

"No, sir."

Delaney couldn't blame her. He wished that he were somewhere else too. He let her enter the communications pod first and then joined her. The message was repeating itself. It was broadcast in stilted English, French, German, Russian and a couple of languages that Delaney didn't recognize.

"Your fleet is gone," it said. "We have destroyed it. Now we will destroy you. Surrender and save your lives. You will be treated well. Fail to surrender and you will die."

Delaney stared at the speaker, suddenly upset by the message, though he didn't know why. The enemy, if he could get Delaney and the regiment to surrender, would not have to fight. That didn't bother him. He'd do the same thing. Make the same threats. That wasn't what bothered him.

"What are we going to do?" asked Soter.

Delaney looked at her as if he hadn't understood. "What?"

"What are we going to do? Will we surrender?"

"No. No, of course not." He rubbed a hand over his face, and said, "If the message changes, let me know."

"Yes, sir."

Delaney left the communications pod and stood for a moment in the bright morning sunlight. It felt good. It reminded him of Earth. And then he understood why he was bothered. The enemy was broadcasting their message in the languages of Earth. Only the languages of Earth. Even those he didn't recognize, he knew were Earth languages. That had to mean the enemy knew who they were facing and probably knew where the home planet was.

He whirled and ran back to the communications pod. "Soter," he yelled. "Prepare a probe. Copy the message from the enemy and then add, they're using only Earth languages. Only Earth. They have to know where our home is."

"Oh my God!"

"Exactly," said Delaney. "They'll head to Earth if we can't stop them."

She spun around and pushed buttons feverishly, copying the

message. She jerked a keyboard toward her and began to type, finished in seconds and then mashed another button. "Probe away," she said.

"Stay with it and keep monitoring."

"Yes, sir."

Delaney ran from the communications pod. He spotted Mony and shouted, "They'll be coming now. Get everyone ready."

As Mony turned to run, the first of the explosions ripped through the camp. The shock wave knocked Delaney from his feet. He hit the ground and rolled over. The air was suddenly hot and oppressive. His ears rang so that he couldn't hear very well.

He rolled over and pushed himself up. He found himself looking at Mony's body. Blood covered the hood of her uniform and a jagged piece of metal was embedded in her throat. He didn't have to check the body to know that she was dead.

He stood up as more bombs fell. He leaped to the right, and rolled over and then down, falling into a shallow depression. There was nothing he could do at the moment. Not with bombs falling. He'd seen or heard no sign of the enemy ships over him. They had to be dropping the weapons from miles above, outside visual range.

There was more explosions. They shook the ground and filled the air with dust and smoke. There was a crackling as beamed weapons swept the defensive perimeter. Delaney kept his face pressed down against the dirt, trying to melt into the ground so that he wouldn't be a target.

He heard one scream and then a second. There was a crackling as someone fired up into the air. It was a useless gesture that Delaney completely understood. It was difficult, almost impossible, to lay in ditches and holes while the enemy fired. He wanted to shoot back, but at the moment there were no targets.

The barrage lasted for fifteen minutes. Bombs and lasers and beams. The ground boiled under the assault. Fires broke out, sweeping through the vegetation. Smoke from the fires filled the air. Now there were more soldiers shouting, driven from their hiding places by the fires.

Delaney rolled over and sat up. He saw his soldiers running, saw them fighting the fires, saw only a few of them watching the sky. Their attention had been diverted.

Delaney leapt up and ran forward shouting. "Half of you back to your positions. Check your weapons. Prepare to receive a ground assault."

He saw the damage done by the bombing. Smoking craters dotted the perimeter. There were a few bodies. The wounded were being treated by the regimental surgeon and the medics.

Delaney looked up into the sky. There was no evidence of the enemy anywhere around. If it hadn't been for the bombing, Delaney would have thought that the enemy had deserted the system.

Everything that could be done was being done. Delaney whirled and ran back to the communications pod. It had been damaged in the bombing but the damage was superficial. Scratches and a single hole in the side. Delaney entered. The equipment seemed to be operating. Soter was sitting on the floor under the overhang of the console, waiting for the bombing to end.

"You need to report all of this. Use a probe. Then record as much information as you can for a burst transmission. When you're ready, send it automatically and then get the hell out of here. They'll probably destroy the pod as soon as the transmission starts."

"We'll lose contact with the fleet," said Soter. She'd made no move to climb from under the console.

"Makes no difference," said Delaney. "We've already lost contact. If the division shows up, they'll be able to find us without the communications pod."

"Yes, sir."

Delaney turned and stepped back outside. The air was split with more sonic booms as ships flashed through the atmosphere overhead, but this time he could see them. Disc-shaped craft that looked as if they could hold fifty or sixty individuals.

Running toward the perimeter, he shouted, *"Get ready! Here they come!"*

Leaping into a crater, he rolled forward, his eyes only inches above the rim. He watched as two of the discs touched down a klick away. Silvery ships with domes on top of them. He saw no opening, but troops began to form on the far side.

Twisting around, Delaney looked at his regiment. The men and women were ready for the attack. He gave the order to fire.

The heavy weapons, the pulse lazer, the particle beams, and even the old-fashioned machine guns began to fire. Beams of light and tracers flashed out. They struck the enemy ship and were absorbed or bounced off.

Delaney wondered about the enemy's tactics. It would seem smarter to land in the center of the camp and let the soldiers attack from the instant they were out of the ships. Why make them charge across open ground where they were vulnerable to everything the regiment could throw at them?

The ships lifted, and as they did, those manning the pulse lasers and the particle beams followed them, firing at them. One ship began to wobble, then one side dipped as the hull began to glow brightly. An instant later it exploded, showering the ground with debris. The shrapnel from the ship cut down some of its own soldiers.

That gave Delaney his answer. Their landing craft were vulnerable from the bottom. Firing up at them could bring them down. He shoved himself away from the crater's rim and ran toward the communications pod. That was a piece of intelligence that could make the difference in a fight.

At the communications pod, Delaney told Soter to prepare the last of the probes with the latest information and fire them all. Then begin the burst transmissions and get the hell out.

"Yes, sir."

Delaney ran from the communications pods as firing erupted along his line. The enemy soldiers were hit but kept coming. The beams were absorbed by their garments or reflected from them. Only a few of them fell. One of them seemed to explode.

It wasn't like an attack on Earth. There wasn't a surging charge of screaming soldiers. They marched forward, not firing, not shouting, not screaming. They came at the regiment, their weapons, if that's what they were, held at port arms. They came in straight lines that didn't waver, no matter how intense the fire became.

Delaney stood watching, wondering. The pulse lasers and the particle beams had not been used. Their crews were scanning the skies, searching for more enemy ships.

"Hit the attackers," Delaney ordered. "Rip them apart."

The pulse lasers opened up, and as they did, the enemy began to die. It was a question of power. They had to overpower the enemy's ability to dissipate the energy. Then one man opened fire with an old-fashioned firearm. An automatic weapon that fired slugs. And that began to rip holes in the enemy's soldiers and his formations. They could deal with lasers and energy weapons, but the old-fashioned rifles and machine guns would kill them quicker.

"Damn," said Delaney. Another piece of information that might help those others out there. He started toward the communications pod so he was looking at it when it vanished. A beam stabbed down out of the clear blue sky, and the pod vanished in a cloud of steam and smoke. He didn't see Soter get clear. She had probably died at her post.

"Damn," he said again.

And then the enemy was on them, firing at them. A thousand of them, walking over the perimeter, using their small weapons that fired a bright green beam that vaporized everything it touched. The only exception was the protective suits that his soldiers wore. For a few seconds, the suits absorbed the energy, but then the circuits overloaded, and the power packs began to detonate.

But his soldiers continued to fight. They grabbed the aliens, threw them to the ground and hammered on them. They used their knives to rip at their suits and then their bodies. They shot them and picked up their weapons, turning the green beams on the enemy.

He saw his troops lift enemy soldiers from their feet and slam them to the ground. He watched as the enemy tried to use hand-to-hand techniques, only to be beaten by the strength and agility of his own soldiers. He saw men and women kick and punch and stab to kill the enemy. He watched them die by the dozens, but there was always more to fill the holes. More enemy ships overhead and more enemy soldiers beginning the walk across the open field.

A dozen of the enemy swarmed over the perimeter and ran right at him. Delaney slipped to one knee and fired his laser rifle. He kept the beam focused on one point until a wisp of smoke appeared and the enemy grabbed at his chest. He fell, screaming in a high-pitched wail, kicking his feet against the hard-packed dirt.

Two of them ran forward. Delaney spun, hit one in the face and heard bone splinter. The creature fell without a sound. Delaney kicked at the second, his foot striking the chest. Again bone splintered and a ragged stain appeared on the alien's uniform. They were fragile opponents, effective only because of their numbers and their technology. On an even footing, it would be no contest.

But there were always more of them. He felt his uniform beginning to heat from the green beam. He fired back, aiming at the big, dark eyes of the enemy soldiers. That one screamed and fell, grabbing at his face, but another began to shoot. Delaney held his trigger down, trying desperately to bleed off the excess energy but knew that it wasn't working. He was beginning to cook inside the suit. If the powerpack didn't detonate, the heat would kill him.

Screaming at the top of his voice, he ran forward, toward the enemy. He kept firing, the beam of his weapon stabbing out, bouncing off targets that ignored him. He reached the one enemy, grabbed him and hurled him away. He kicked at a second and clubbed a third with his fist, all the time aware that someone was hitting him with a beam. He heard the overload warning on his powerpack and knew that he could do nothing about it.

Standing among a half dozen of the enemy, he waited for the detonation. The explosion, the resulting shrapnel, would kill some of them. It was the final act of a desperate man. Take as many of them with him as possible.

He was aware of a moment of blinding pain and then the horrible realization that it was all over. His regiment was dead. If there was a single comforting thought, it was that the enemy had not captured the regimental colors. They had burned as the fleet had plunged into the atmosphere. He would not suffer the ultimate defeat of losing both his regiment and its colors.

That was his final thought.

7

FLAGSHIP OF THE TENTH INTERPLANETARY INFANTRY REGIMENT

"I DON'T LIKE it," said Captain Jack Clemens. He was older than most of the people on the ship, had graying hair and brown eyes. His features were narrow, he had a pointed nose and a graceful, almost feminine neck. He sat in the captain's chair facing the view screen that showed the space around his craft. "I don't like it at all."

Jefferson was standing to one side, aware of the others on the bridge, the technicians, the officers, the navigator and the helmsman. He was aware of them trying to look as if they weren't listening.

"We're going to need every minute we can get on the planet's surface. I know this will burn up fuel and it's a strain on your crew, but I think it's necessary."

"Why now?" asked Clemens.

"Because contact has been lost with the Eighth. That might mean nothing, but it could mean everything. We'll be in a better position if we can get to the Eighty-two Eridani system sooner."

"It'll take about four hours to get ready," said Clemens.

"Fine. Anything special I should do for my people?"

"Walking around is going to be next to impossible. Feed

them and have them relieve themselves before we begin the acceleration," said Clemens. "Use the individual disposible hygiene units. Once we begin we're not going to shut it down."

"No problem," said Jefferson.

"We're not going to gain much time this way. I think you could use the trip time better with training, not laying around feeling as if you weigh six hundred pounds."

"That's my problem," said Jefferson.

"It sure is, Colonel. I don't suppose I have to tell you to make sure that your people are lying flat, that they must remain in their individual cubes, in the webbing and to be careful that there is nothing hard under them."

"What about those who don't have individual cubes?" asked Jefferson.

"They need to be on a flat surface with some kind of padding under them. Make sure that there are no wrinkles or lumps under them that might shut off the blood supply to a limb."

Jefferson nodded. "Four hours, you say."

"We'll be ready in four hours," said Clemens.

"Thank you, Captain." Jefferson left the bridge and walked toward the mid-lift. He took it down, exited and then headed toward the regimental headquarters. There he found Martha Simms, one of the clerks.

"I want a staff meeting in ten minutes. Include Colonel Davies and her people too."

"Yes, sir."

"I'm going to find Captain Carter. I'll be in intell and then move to the conference room. I'll be there in ten minutes."

"Yes, sir."

Jefferson left, wondering if he was doing the right thing. The troops were going to have to stay on their backs for a couple of hours or so. No one could move without endangering himself or herself. With the weight of three or four gravities, it was easy to break bones. It was easy to rip muscles and it was easy to kill yourself. Too much could go wrong.

But lying there with nothing to do except think was hard on the troops. They knew they were heading into battle. Maybe not in a week or a month, but soon, and soldiers who had nothing to do except think scared themselves easily.

And that wasn't even thinking about the discomfort, the fighting for every breath, and the lying around in what was euphemistically called a personal disposal hygiene unit but was nothing more than a diaper for adults.

You couldn't eat, it was almost impossible to talk because it took so much effort. They sometimes could pipe in music or some kind of audio drama to help pass the time, but that was only if the ship's company thought of it. Sometimes they didn't. Besides, they were as uncomfortable as the soldiers. The gravity, the weight, was the same for them, but they had work to do as well.

Jefferson found Carter sitting in the intell office where he'd left him. As he entered, he asked, "Anything new coming in?"

"No, sir. You can't expect anything soon either. We're now a couple of light years from the divisional ships and more than a couple from the Alpha Mensae system. We need a courier or one of the drones to rendezvous with us. Nothing coming in."

"When do you expect the next courier?" asked Jefferson.

"I never expect them, Colonel. You should have a better feel for that than I do."

Jefferson nodded. "You worried about the lack of communication with the Eighth?"

"Honestly? Yes, sir, I am. I think they're in deep trouble and there's nothing we can do about it. We'll soon be in the same boat. On the ground with no help around us. It'll be up to us to succeed or fail right there."

"I don't need a lecture on that," said Jefferson.

"No, sir, I guess you don't."

"I'm calling a staff meeting in about seven minutes. You are excused."

"Yes, sir."

When Jefferson reached the conference room, everyone was there except for Colonel Davies. As Jefferson entered, he was told that she would be there in a moment.

Jefferson nodded and walked to the head of the table and sat down. He looked at the faces of the men and women surrounding him and saw that no one looked too happy. They all looked tired and it wasn't just from putting together the games. It was the stress of the oncoming enemy and the uncertainty of what was going to happen in the next few weeks. And it was the strain of knowing that Earth was at risk. Sometimes soldiers could ignore their own danger, but when their homes were in the path of the enemy, things changed. Soldiers began to worry about their homes and families.

He pulled himself back to reality and looked at Torrence. "Before we start, what are the daily results of the games?"

Torrence looked at him like he'd lost his mind. "The games? You called a staff meeting for that?"

"Major," said Jefferson quietly, "I called the meeting for other reasons, but until Colonel Davies is here, we can't start. The games results."

"Yes, sir. Our battalions who have run combat proficiency tests are slightly ahead of the Seventh. They, on the other hand, are slightly ahead in the rifle competition. No one has run the assault course."

"In other words," said Jefferson, "we're about tied on this?"

"Yes, sir. I wouldn't want to have to bet on who is ahead overall right now."

"Good," said Jefferson. "We'll announce that the results are virtually tied."

Davies entered then. She took an empty chair and said, "Sorry. A couple of last-minute details."

Jefferson nodded and said, "I've called you here to let you know that we have about four hours. Then Captain Clemens is going to begin to accelerate so that we can get to Eighty-two Eridani faster."

"That necessary?" asked one of the officers.

Jefferson shrugged. "At the moment, we just don't know, but I think it's important that we get there as quickly as possible. Every hour we can buy might make the difference. We'll be that much better prepared."

"The question remains," said the officer.

"The answer is that the Eighth has missed some of their check-in times. We don't know if that is significant, but I don't want to take the chance. I want us to get into position," said Jefferson.

"What do we have to do?" asked Davies.

"Get the troops ready for the acceleration. Make sure that loose equipment is tied down, and then let Clemens and the navy take care of business."

Torrence interrupted. "We don't have anything firm, do we? Could it just be a communications problem?"

Jefferson nodded and then said, "But it's a chance we don't have to take. The extra time will let us prepare better defensive positions." He hesitated and then said, "Besides, it relieves the tension between our two regiments. No one is going to get into trouble at three or four times normal gravity."

"There anything definite?"

"No," said Jefferson. "It's guesswork now. I've got Carter, my intelligence officer, trying to determine something, but I don't think that's going to happen. We're just going to have to make the best guesses possible." He looked around the table. "There any questions?"

The officers sat there quietly, each knowing exactly what had to be done. It wasn't necessary for them to ask questions. Jefferson nodded at them and said, "We'll meet again, as soon as possible, and get the final briefings before planet fall." He stood up. "Good luck to you all."

Torrence said, "Thank you, sir."

When everyone was ready for the acceleration, Jefferson retreated to his cabin. His roommate was already there, lying on his bed, strapped in, waiting for the beginning. He looked up when Jefferson entered, but said nothing.

Jefferson sat down at the computer, used the keyboard for a moment and then turned the screen so that he'd be able to see it from his cot. He'd keyed it into the main screen on the bridge so that he'd be able to see everything that Clemens did, and if there were any messages, or the recovery of any probes, or the landing of a courier, he'd know it.

Satisfied with that, Jefferson touched the keypad and said, "Captain Clemens, we're ready when you are."

"Thank you, Colonel. We will begin the acceleration in ten minutes."

Jefferson sat for a moment, not sure of what he should say

now. He felt the urge to say something more, but couldn't think of what it would be. Finally, he said, "You may begin now."

"Yes, sir," said Clemens.

Jefferson moved to his cot, stripped off his boots and then lay back.

"Do we really need to do this, Colonel?" asked Montgomery, quietly.

"I think so," said Jefferson. He nearly snapped out the answer because he was tired of having his decision questioned, but then Montgomery hadn't been at the staff meeting. "Yeah, I think so."

There was a quiet bong at the hatch. Jefferson glanced at the computer but it was set for a relay from the main screen on the bridge. He'd have to get up to use the keypad to learn who it was.

But then the hatch opened and Davies hurried in. She saw that both Jefferson and Montgomery were ready for the acceleration.

"We've only got a couple of minutes," said Jefferson.

"I know." She hurried toward him and sat down on his cot. "Move over."

"I don't think the entire command structure of the regiments should be in the same place," said Jefferson.

"It's not. My exec and yours are somewhere else. Besides, what could happen?"

Jefferson thought of a dozen things that could happen, from the cot collapsing under their combined weight to a hole in the hull that would allow the air to escape from their section before they could do a thing about it. There were accidents that they could neither anticipate nor prevent. It didn't make sense to have both commanding officers in the same location.

"Move over," she said, pushing on him.

Over the ship's intercom came, "We have one minute to acceleration. One minute to acceleration."

"No time now," she said.

Jefferson slipped over giving her room on the cot. He felt it shift as she lay back and then felt the warmth of her thigh, hip and shoulder against his.

"This isn't going to work," he said.

"Nothing to work. Now we have the opportunity to discuss the deployment on the planet while the ship accelerates."

Jefferson shook his head, wishing that the woman next to him was Torrence and not Davies. Davies was a fellow officer, fellow commanding officer, and he'd never thought about her as a woman. Not the way he sometimes thought about Torrence.

"Thirty seconds," said the mechanical voice. "Thirty seconds."

"Too late now," said Davies, wiggling slightly as if to get comfortable.

"Sorry I'm here to spoil the fun," said Montgomery, grinning at them.

"There will be no fun under three or four gravities," said Jefferson. But the thought was put in his mind. Naturally they couldn't lie one on top of the other, but front to back or front to front on the side would work. Maybe. It might be an interesting experiment.

He forced the thought from his mind. That was the last thing he needed to do. They were on their way into a hostile environment to meet a hostile force. He didn't need to have his judgment clouded by ridiculous thoughts of sex under the pressure of three or four gravities.

The announcement came. "Ten seconds. Prepare for acceleration in five seconds. Four. Three. Two. One. Acceleration."

"I don't feel anything," said Davies.

And then slowly, the pressure built. Jefferson thought he could hear the rumbling of the engines. Or maybe it was a vibration as the power built and the ship began to increase its speed.

"Now I do," said Davies. "Hard to breathe."

Jefferson was now more aware of her lying beside him. The light pressure from her body was now a heavy presence. He wished that she wasn't there. He wished that he was alone on the cot.

"How long?" she asked.

"As long as it takes," said Jefferson.

Clemens had tilted his command chair back. He could still see the main screen, and with the controls recessed into the arms of his chair, he could change the view, he could control the engines, and he could fire the weapons. It wasn't the ideal situation, but it was all that could be done.

The bridge staff had been reduced to those essential for the operation of the ship. The helmsman, navigator and the communications officer were still there. The science officer, the engineer, and the medical officer had headed to other parts of the ship to complete their duties.

Each of the men and women on the bridge wore suits that could be inflated in moments. It would relieve some of the pressure, and it would allow them to move with relative safety if it became necessary.

Clemens turned his head slowly and watched the display as the speed of the ship increased, slowly at first. After fifteen minutes, the rate of acceleration became constant, holding them at just under four gravities. He turned his attention back to the main view screen, watching as the stars became little more than blurs of light.

"Sensor sweeps confirm our path is clear."

"Thank you," said Clemens. "Communications, have you received anything?"

"No, sir. Radios are silent. We're leaving the division behind us at more than the speed of light."

"I understand that, but we're moving, more or less, toward the Earth."

"Nothing from that quarter," said the communications officer.

Clemens tried to take a deep breath but found it was more work than it was worth. He kept his breathing shallow, sucking at the air quickly as sweat beaded on his forehead and dripped. Now the beads were not the light, flyweight touch on his face and body. They felt like flattened pebbles being pushed down against his skin.

He hoped that nothing would happen for the next few hours. He hoped that everything would progress normally because it was difficult to react to emergencies at four gravities. And he hoped that everyone had gotten strapped in or fastened in before the acceleration started.

"How long?" asked the navigator.

"Couple of hours," said Clemens. "A couple of hours."

8

ABOARD THE SS *CARL SPAATZ*

THE SCOUT STOOD in the general's conference room facing the staff and the general himself. The scout, called Kit Carson by his friends because Kit Carson was the greatest scout they knew, was a thin man. His uniform was wrinkled and smelled. That was the result of days in space, in his one-man ship, where there was no space to move and no space for a change of clothes. The scouts had one job. They went out, looked around and came back. At very high speed. They could do in a day what a normal ship did in a month. High-speed recon was their function and they did it very well.

Carson didn't move, standing at a relaxed attention, and waited for someone to tell him what to do. He'd learned long ago not to volunteer the information in the order he thought it should be told. Generals had different priorities. Carson let the general decide.

"You've come from there?" asked the general.

"Yes, sir. I didn't have much time to look around. The system was swarming with enemy ships. With what . . . hell, looked like the flying saucers everyone used to report on old Earth."

"Did you get close to the planet?"

"Well, sir, I got close enough to know that there were no radio signals coming from it."

"Visual?"

"Records are being downloaded from my ship now," said Carson. "I came directly here. No time for a drink or a piss. Right to the conference room."

The general nodded and said, "What did you see?"

"Alpha Mensae was alive with the enemy. Fifty, sixty ships out there. Some on picket duty, I imagine, but space is a big place and a little ship that doesn't emit electromagnetic radiation, that drifts in, is very hard to spot."

"Yes, yes," said the general.

"Once I had penetrated the outer ring of their pickets, they weren't really looking for intruders. I worked my way in toward the planet. As I entered the biosphere, I saw an increase in the enemy ships. Maybe a dozen of them in parking orbits above the planet. I couldn't use my scanners or sensors, radio or radar. That would have told them I was there."

The general was losing patience. "I know that. Just tell me what you did observe."

"Seemed that the planet was crawling with them. No sign of our people. No evidence that they were still on the planet's surface. No evidence that there were any survivors down there at all."

"Good God," said Prescott. "A whole regiment."

Carson looked at him and shrugged. "Looks like."

"Jesus. The whole regiment. Gone."

Carson turned his attention back to the general. "I stayed as long as I could. Now, they might have moved our people off the planet, or might have captured some of them and held them somewhere on the planet. That I don't know. But the Alpha Mensae now belongs to the enemy, and it'd take everything we have here to make any kind of an assault on them. And then I don't know if we could do it without help."

"We can't just write those people off," said one of the officers.

"Why not?" asked the general. "Right now, there is nothing that we can do for them, if they still live. We can't sacrifice the division on the assumption that some of our people are still alive."

"Then," said the officer, "you'll never get anyone to follow your orders. If they know that you'll abandon them, they'll never fight for you."

"No," said the general, his voice cutting through the air like a knife. "They'll fight because they know that nothing stands between the Earth and those barbarians. They'll fight because their homes are at peril. And they'll fight, knowing we might abandon them, and they won't care because they'll know we're doing it for the good of Earth."

"There's nothing we can do for them now," said Carson. "Nothing at all but get a lot of people killed."

"Later," said the general, "when the Earth is safe and the enemy's on the run, we'll get our people. We'll find out what happened to them, but right now the protection of Earth has to take priority."

"Yes, General," said the officer.

"It's the best we can do for them," he said. "It's all we can do for them. They knew the score when they signed up."

"Yes, sir."

The general turned his attention back on Carson. "Please. Continue."

"I made as much of a survey as I could, looking for our radio signature, looking for anything that showed a large concentration of humans. Passive, of course. Maybe with the instruments available here, and with no restraints on the systems used, we could find something. I couldn't risk it."

"The fleet?" said the naval officer present. A young lieutenant commander named George Simons who drew the duty of liaison officer.

"I'm sorry," said Carson, "but I saw no fleet. There was some debris around the planet that could have been a fleet, or the remains of one."

"Nothing that you could identify?" asked Simons.

"Clouds of floating junk with no pieces much larger than a silver dollar."

"Oh, Christ. Nothing there at all?"

"The question has been answered," said the general. "If the fleet had escaped, radio or probes would have alerted us. We must assume that all ships have been lost."

"Christ!"

Carson looked around the room slowly. He had just informed them that a regiment and its supporting fleet had been eliminated and they displayed almost no emotion. It was as if he'd announced that the home team had lost a single, unimportant game.

And then he realized that was exactly what he'd announced. The home team had lost an unimportant game. The Alpha Mensae system meant nothing to the people of Earth. It hadn't been colonized, there were no humans living there now, and if the enemy held it, no one on Earth would care. The real test would come as they tried to hold the next line of defense.

"Captain Carson," said the general. "I want you to immediately take a report to Colonel Jefferson and Colonel Davies heading for the Eighty-Two Eridani system. They need to know what has happened."

"Yes, sir. How soon?"

"How soon what?"

"How soon do you want me to take the report?"

The general looked at Carson for a moment and said, "Right away, of course."

"I've just come out of space . . . I've just . . . "

"It is the price of being a scout," said the general. Then he thought better of it. "Get a shower, clean clothes and some hot food. We'll prepare a report and it'll be ready for transmission in . . . twelve hours. You be ready then."

"Yes, sir."

The pressure of the acceleration decreased gradually, so slowly at first that no one noticed it. There was a quiet bong and an announcement. "Acceleration ending. Remain in place until the captain has completed his maneuvering."

Jefferson turned his head slightly and saw that Davies was staring up at the overhead. Her eyes blinked in what looked to be slow motion.

Slowly he turned to look at Montgomery. The officer hadn't moved or spoken in hours. The center of his cot sagged and there was bright blood on his uniform.

"Montgomery," said Jefferson slowly, trying to focus his eyes. "Are you all right?"

There was no answer.

Jefferson forced himself to roll to his side. The pressure from gravity was sliding away. He lifted his head enough to see blood pooling on the deck under the bunk. Jefferson struggled to sit up, made it and then tried to stand. The effort left him breathing heavily, the sweat staining his uniform.

"What is it?" asked Davies, her voice slurred.

"Montgomery has been injured." Looking down at the blood, Jefferson was sure the man was dead. Too much blood for him to have survived.

Jefferson forced his way to the deck, feeling like an old man who had been confined to his bed for a month. His muscles didn't respond as they should. He seemed weak, unsteady, and thought that he was going to pass out from the effort. He dropped into the plastic chair and heard a quiet snap as it took his weight.

Reaching forward, he hit the keypad and said, "We need a medic to Jefferson's cabin. Sick bay, we need a medic."

There was a moment of silence and then, "Is it an emergency?"

Jefferson shot a glance at the prone, motionless body and said, "No. It's not an emergency."

"We'll be there when we can then."

Jefferson caught the frantic tone of the voice. "What's happened?"

"We have a number of injured. We're working on them as fast as we can."

"Any dead?"

"Wait one."

Jefferson sat staring at the screen that still showed the space outside the ship. He hadn't bothered to switch the computer over.

"We've four confirmed dead now."

"Shit," said Jefferson.

Davies said, "Find out which regiment."

Jefferson turned to look at her. She was sitting on the edge of the cot, her head bowed, looking as if she had just run a marathon.

Then he noticed that it was easier to move. The gravity was returning to normal. The air didn't feel leaden anymore.

"That's not important at the moment. We've got to let them do their job."

She got up and walked around to the other cot. She reached down and felt for a pulse at Montgomery's throat. Nothing. No sign of life.

"Dead," she said.

"I thought so. Makes it five."

The report was on a computer disk that fit into his pocket. Not much weight to it. A plastic square that contained everything that general staff knew about the enemy and the fight in the Alpha Mensae system. Carson had been told that someone had recovered a probe that had been launched by Delaney on the planet's surface. It provided some information. They hadn't shared it with him. Just told him to give it to Colonel Jefferson as soon as he could.

Carson walked slowly down to the shuttle bay where his scout craft had been serviced by the maintenance crews there. He didn't bother with the pre-flight because he knew that the maintenance crew had done a better job of it than he could. They were taught the tolerances allowed in the moving parts, they knew how the electrical systems worked, and they understood the mechanics of spaceflight. Carson didn't and couldn't have cared less. As long as the ship got him where he was going, he didn't care how it did it.

He opened the hatch that led into the cockpit. He pulled himself through it and then settled himself into the wrap-around seat. It was molded to his body. The inner parts were filled with a thick, gelatinous substance that absorbed the shock of massive acceleration. With a helmet on, a facemask feeding him oxygen, there was almost no discomfort from the acceleration. Almost none.

Carson settled himself into the seat and looked at the instrument array in front of him. Right in the center was a view screen that showed him the stars in front of him or behind him or over him. With the touch of a button he could change the view. Other instruments, sensors, scanners, radars, infrared cameras, gave him a wide variety of different information.

Of course, set across the top were the flight instruments.

They told him how fast, in what direction and for how long. To the right were the supplies that he'd need to survive. Food capsules and water. To the left were the flight controls. It was set up that way because Carson was left-handed.

He could exercise, if he wanted, by artificially changing the tension in the seat and then pressing back against it as hard as he could. There was no way for him to stand, but by rotating the seat, he could stretch out. After two or three days, it became uncomfortable, but he was rarely out for two or three days. Normally there was a chance to land, get out and walk about. Normally.

He settled the helmet on his head and touched one of the buttons. "Control, how do you copy?"

"We have you loud and clear. Are you ready?"

Carson grinned and said, "Negative. Give me five minutes to run the diagnostic checks."

"Roger that."

Carson reached up and used the keyboard, telling the craft to look at itself. It was to make sure that all systems were up and operating and that all hatches, access doors, and instrument ports were closed for the launch.

When everything was flashing green, Carson radioed the control. "I'm up and ready to roll."

"Roger. We're opening the main doors now. Stand by for start sequence."

"Standing by." He watched as the APU lights came on. The external power connection was made. Carson started the engine but held it at the low idle setting.

"Doors open," said control.

The lights in the shuttle bay, except for a single bank of red, were extinguished. On the screen, it looked as if it was high noon. He could easily see the other craft, the technicians in their protective suits working around him.

"APU disconnect."

"Roger disconnect," said Carson. He watched as a technician dragged the APU away from his ship.

"You're cleared to exit shuttle bay."

"Wait one," said Carson. He reached up and ran a finger along a series of press-to-test lights, making sure that all the connections were solid. Satisfied, he keyed his mike again. "Lifting off."

"Roger."

Carson turned his ship so that it was facing the main door. When the nose was centered, he pushed his stick forward, feeling the ship begin to slide. The scene on the screen changed as he neared the door. Beyond it was nothing but empty space.

"Good luck," said the controller.

"Thanks. Tell the general I said good-bye."

"Roger."

Carson cleared the doors and hit the button. His ship began a gradual acceleration. He touched the nav button, watched as the scene on the screen changed. He turned slightly, until the red dot that marked his destination was centered in the screen. When it was, he pushed himself back in the seat and then engaged the thrusters. The ship leaped forward like it had been kicked. He was slightly aware of the sudden acceleration.

Satisfied that the ship was on the right course, as programmed by the computers on the divisional ship, and that nothing was going to happen to him in the next few minutes, Carson turned on the cassette player, letting the rock and roll of another age drift over him. That was the one modification that he'd insisted on. If he was going to travel great distances by himself, he wanted the music to go with him. Others had videos or computer books, but Carson had wanted the music. Which was not to say he couldn't dial up a video or a book if the mood moved him.

He checked the instruments carefully, saw that everything was still in the green and relaxed. It was going to be a long trip. There was nothing he could do but relax and enjoy it while his equipment kept him on the right path, kept the ship from exploding and kept him entertained as best it could.

"Nothing to worry about," he said out loud, but the words were muffled by the facemask he wore. Even with that, life was beautiful because there was no one around to hassle him.

9

FLAGSHIP OF THE TENTH INTERPLANETARY INFANTRY REGIMENT

THERE HAD BEEN twelve people killed during the acceleration. They died because equipment failed, or broke, or they were careless. They died because a small injury at normal gravity was more severe at four times normal gravity, and they died because they didn't have the strength to call for help once they realized they were in trouble. They let the life drain from themselves under the crushing burden of the extra gravity.

Jefferson had decided that he didn't want to remain in the cabin with a dead man. He'd seen bodies before. Combat created a large number of bodies, but in combat there wasn't much that he could do about it. Here, he could. Here, he could head up to the bridge to learn what was going on.

"You want to stay for the medics?" asked Jefferson.

Davies looked at Montgomery and shrugged. "Makes no difference to me, though I should check on my troops."

"I'll take care of that."

She thought about it for a moment and then said, "I'd better check with my exec."

Jefferson pointed at the computer. "You can do it right there."

"Fine. I'll stay."

"Good." Jefferson opened the hatch and nearly bolted into the corridor. He was surprised to find it nearly dark, only a few red lights burning along it and then realized, with the ship in acceleration, there wouldn't be people moving around. No reason to waste energy lighting corridors that no one would use.

He walked to the mid-lift and took it to the bridge. He got off to find the reduced staff there. Clemens was sitting in his chair, staring at the screen.

"We're going to have to decelerate pretty soon," said Clemens without preamble. "If we don't, we'll overshoot our target."

"How'd things go with the acceleration?"

Clemens shrugged. "You've got the reports, I'm sure. We've some dead and injured but no structural damage." He turned and looked at Jefferson. "I hope the speed was worth the cost."

"I don't know if it will be," said Jefferson. He didn't know whether he should be angry or sad. Twelve dead so that he could arrive at the destination earlier. But that extra time might make all the difference. At the moment there was no way to tell.

"Deceleration will be as bad," said Clemens.

Jefferson stepped down into the forward section of the bridge. He walked toward the view screen. The stars were blurred because of the speed of the ship. Little blobs of light shoved into a corner of the view screen.

"Which one is Eighty-two Eridani?" he asked.

The navigator pointed. "That one there."

"Seems as far away as the others," said Jefferson.

"We're still talking several light years," said Clemens. "It's a sun-class star so it's not going to shine like Sirius."

"Still . . . "

"In the next few hours, as we get closer to it," said the navigator, "it'll begin to grow. There'll be a marked difference in it. You'll see."

Jefferson turned back to Clemens. "When do you plan to begin the deceleration?"

"Ten, twelve hours," he said. "That'll put us into the system in about three days' time."

Jefferson stood for a moment and then turned back to the flatscreen, staring at it. It looked like a hammered silver tray with glowing marbles in one corner. Nothing interesting to see. Nothing that looked like the night sky he'd seen on a dozen different planets. Just lousy reception on a poor television monitor.

"I'll be meeting with my staff in the main conference room for the next few hours. Company grade officers and senior NCOs will be responsible for getting the troops ready for the deceleration."

"I'll keep you posted," said Clemens.

Jefferson sat at the head of the table and looked at the senior staff officers from both regiments and wondered what in the hell they were doing there. He seemed to have fallen into the trap that too many senior officers blundered into. When in doubt, when there was nothing else scheduled, hold a meeting.

The silence hung heavy in the air and all eyes were on him, expecting him to do something or to say something. Jefferson sat there, sweat beading on his forehead and face, dripping to the collar of his uniform.

Finally he said, "Captain Carter, do you have a briefing package prepared on Eighty-two Eridani?"

"Yes, sir." He used the buttons in front of him to call up a holographic display of the planetary system of Eighty-two Eridani.

Jefferson tuned Carter out. He knew about the planet and the system, having heard it all from the general's intelligence officer a few days earlier. Only a few days? It seemed so long ago. So much had been crammed into so few hours.

"Biological probes," said Carter.

Jefferson blinked once and looked at his intelligence officer. His earlier briefing had skirted that issue. Jefferson had thought they were landing on a planet filled with vegetation but no animal life. At least Carter hadn't said anything about animal life.

"Biological probes," repeated Carter, "have indicated lush

vegetation, much of it looking Earth-normal. Recent studies, however, have detected animal life that looks suspiciously like the dinosaurs that once walked the Earth."

"Good God!" said Torrence. "You mean we've found the Lost World?"

Carter shrugged. "That is the latest data."

The medical officer of the Seventh, an older woman with long, graying hair and bright blue eyes, said, "If the vegetation is close to Earth-normal, or if it could live in an Earth-like environment, we might have trouble with disease."

"Are you sure?" asked Jefferson.

"No, Colonel, I'm not. I'm merely saying that there is that possibility. You might have heard, or read, how the diseases of the European invaders in the New World nearly eliminated the native populations."

"Vaccinations?" asked Jefferson.

"Against what?" asked the medical officer. "I have no idea what we might encounter. If the diseases can infect our troops, I would imagine that some of our antibodies will be able to knock them out. But there is always the possibility that we'll find a new, deadly disease that we have no way of combating."

"Won't there be an incubation period?" asked Torrence.

"Maybe. Maybe not. We can speculate all day long and never come up with an answer." She looked from face to face. "Odds are that we'll encounter no such diseases. We've explored a hundred planets, many with Earth-type conditions, and we've yet to encounter a deadly disease . . . with the exception of Tears Pathology. Simple penicillin knocked it out, but not before nearly thirty thousand people contracted it and about a third of them died."

Jefferson asked, "What are you advocating?"

"When we deploy, we deploy with a fully equipped medical lab. My people have one prepared already, and it would only need the use of a single shuttle."

Jefferson rubbed his face slowly, looked at the sweat on his fingers and then wiped them on the front of his uniform. "I'll want my medical officer to look at it to make sure that you've covered all the bases."

"Yes, sir. Glad to have the assistance."

Jefferson turned his attention back to Carter. "You said dinosaurs?"

"Yes, sir, I did."

"Dinosaurs?"

"Well, sir, we don't know that much about the fauna on the planet. I've looked at the preliminary colonial surveys, and they don't mention anything about large animals, but hell, as fast as some of those are accomplished, I'm not surprised."

"They a danger to us?"

"Any large animal can be a threat. Hell, elephants aren't particularly belligerent, but they sure as hell can stomp you flat if the urge hits them."

"Point taken," said Jefferson. "Besides, we're not on an environmental crusade here. Anyone runs into a large animal that even looks dangerous, take it out."

"Yes, sir," said Torrence.

Jefferson looked at the hologram still hanging in the air above the conference table. Their target planet looked insignificant against the backdrop of the Eighty-two Eridani solar system. A small planet that had no real oceans, but had large continents covered with thick vegetation. It had to be a delicate balance. A little too much water and the low-lying areas would fill, choking the growth there. Not quite enough and portions could turn into desert.

The officers were discussing the deployment, talking about the same things they always talked about. Order of deployment, mission of the first soldiers on the ground, who would have the task of guarding the airhead and who would have the task of erecting the structures, under the guidance of the combat engineers. Those were logisitical problems that didn't interest Jefferson. He sat there and listened, ready to end the disputes, if any erupted.

There was a quiet bong on the command circuit, and Jefferson looked down at the recessed screen. Clemens's face was there. When he saw he had Jefferson's attention, he said, "We've picked up a ship coming at us."

"Single ship?"

"Yes. Small. Signature is of one of our scout craft."

"Rate of closure?"

"He'll be here in nine or ten hours."

"If we wait for him before beginning the deceleration, how will that affect our schedule?"

"I don't think it'll make that much difference. We might have to brake a little harder but that would be it."

"Then let's recover the scout before the deceleration."

"Yes, sir." The screen went blank.

Jefferson turned to the rest of the staff. "If there is nothing pressing here, I suggest that we adjourn for a couple of hours. Captain Clemens has informed me that a courier is inbound. He may have new information for us."

When no one said a word, Jefferson stood. "Let's get everything ready for the deceleration and then have something to eat. We'll meet here as soon as the courier is aboard."

Without waiting for a response, Jefferson headed for the hatch.

Carson couldn't believe the speed the fleet was making. He'd had to increase his power a couple of times because it didn't seem that he was catching them. It had seemed to him that he was standing still and they were flying away from him. But slowly the angles changed, and he realized that he'd overcompensated.

He sat quietly for a moment, the rock and roll blaring, filling the tiny ship. He ignored that as he touched the controls, fired a rocket to slow himself, and then another to change his direction slightly.

Radio would do him no good for the moment. The broadcast would be left behind as he raced through the sky. Communications with the ship would be impossible until the ranges changed.

He aimed at the middle of the flagship, obvious because of its size. The other vessels were escort ships, cruisers and destroyers designed to protect the flagship in much the same way that smaller ships of the old water navies surrounded and protected the aircraft carriers.

He was sure he had been detected. The fleet would have pickets out, but he could spot none of them. And if they had spotted him, they would know that he wasn't much of a threat.

A single small ship could, in a suicide attack, slam into the flagship to destroy it, but the weapons systems on it would bring him under fire lock before he could harm them. He was at their mercy and they knew he was coming.

But, as he approached, he saw that no attempt was made to stop him. The lights around the hanger doors came on, first glowing bright red to keep him away, and finally switching over to green. The doors opened slowly and he could see the brightness of the interior.

Now the radio came alive with instructions, telling him what he needed to know to land, but also asking for his IFF. They wanted to make sure that they were not allowing an enemy vessel to land on their hangar deck.

Carson touched a button and the automatic IFF responded to their interrogation. Nothing changed on the flagship, telling him that his responses had been correct.

Then suddenly, over the radio, he heard, "Scout, you are cleared to make you final approach and landing."

"Roger," he said, not sure that they'd heard his acknowledgment before he began aligning his ship.

He worked to match the speed of the flagship, hanging half a klick behind it. He watched the lights on the door, knowing that what he was seeing was an event that was thirty seconds or so in the past. He was aiming at a ship that had moved beyond that point.

Once he had his speed adjusted, he touched the controls and began to slide forward slowly even though he was still moving faster than the speed of light. He let the situation stabilize. The last thing he could afford was to run out of patience. Sometimes it took an hour or two to dock. That was better than suddenly finding yourself inside the hangar with far too much forward speed.

He aimed at the center of the glowing green lights. He moved forward carefully, watching for signs that he had picked up too much forward speed. It was a tricky thing. On Earth, on an old-fashioned aircraft carrier, no one thought about the attraction of the two objects. The force of gravity generated by the carrier was so small that pilots never considered it. But in space, the attraction was enough to create real trouble if the pilot wasn't careful.

So Carson had to be careful, sliding forward, watching the lights, watching the readings on his instruments and listening to the directions from the ship's control. He needed all the information to make a landing at translight speed.

Angles changed slightly, and Carson made the tiny corrections, just caressing the controls as he'd been taught so long ago. Think about the correction without really making it. Let the senses and the fingers take over. Let the ship slide forward and don't get impatient. That would kill quicker than anything else.

And suddenly the perspective changed radically, and Carson realized that he had entered the doors. He was now part of the large ship. He was now wrapped in its protection. He reduced the power and let the ship drift down to rest on the hangar deck. As it touched down, he cut his engines. He no longer needed them. He'd made it.

Maintenance crews rushed out to secure his ship. They wore protective gear since there was no air on the hangar deck at the moment. He touched a button and had a rearview on the screen. Now he could see the doors beginning to close. All he could do was sit there and wait.

Using the screen again, he noticed the armed guards on the deck. That seemed ridiculous. If he were an enemy agent, he would detonate the ship where it was. No need to get out. And he could act before the guards would know to shoot him. If he were an enemy.

A few moments later the hatch popped as the maintenance crew worked to extract him. The cold air rushed up into his ship and that seemed to revive him. It woke him up. He peeled the facemask away, stripped his helmet and began the task of climbing out of the scout ship.

"You okay, pal?" shouted someone.

"Yeah," yelled Carson back. "Just stiff." He found that prying himself out of the seat was getting tougher. The muscles no longer had the resilience of the young. His joints popped and his muscles screamed. He was getting too old for the scouting business.

He levered himself into the accessway and felt hands on his body, helping him out. He felt his feet on the deck, slid forward slightly and ducked his head so that he could stand up. It seemed overly bright on the hangar deck. He was used to the subdued lighting in the ship.

"Captain wants to see you right away," said one of the maintenance men.

"No time to take a piss or grab a Coke?"

"Captain wants you now. We've got to begin deceleration as quickly as we can."

"Right," said Carson. He hurried to the hatch, let the guard open it, and found himself being escorted to the bridge. There never was time for a piss or a Coke.

10

FLAGSHIP OF THE TENTH INTERPLANETARY INFANTRY REGIMENT

CARSON REACHED THE bridge and was allowed to enter without the escort. He saw the ship's captain sitting in his chair, looking at the screen which showed him nothing that he recognized.

"Captain?" said Carson.

The officer turned and nodded. "Clemens. And you are?"

"Carson. Everyone calls me Kit for obvious reasons."

"Well, Mister Carson, I hope that you planned to stay with us for a while. We've got to begin deceleration immediately or overshoot our destination."

"I have important intelligence," said Carson.

Clemens held out a hand. "Give it to me."

"I'm supposed to deliver it Colonel Jefferson."

"I'll see that it is plugged into the computer system," said Clemens.

Carson hesitated for a moment and then said, "Certainly, Captain." He pulled the disk from his pocket and handed it to Clemens.

"Thank you. Now, we'd better get you ready for the deceleration."

"Yes, sir."

Carson turned, saw his escort and hurried off the bridge. They walked down a corridor and the escort opened a door. "You'll find a cot in there."

"Thanks," said Carson.

"We're going to start the deceleration in about five or ten minutes. There'll be a warning and then a countdown."

"I'm aware of the procedure," said Carson.

"Fine."

Carson walked into the cabin, looked at the cot and stripped the sheet and blanket from it quickly. He tossed them to the deck and then sat down. He pulled his boots off, then his socks and finally completely unbuttoned his shirt. He lay back thinking that he just loved going from one restrictive environment to another. At least he wasn't stuck in his tiny scout ship and that was something.

Jefferson, lying on his cot, thought that he was getting nothing done. All he could do was run from one thing to the next and then stop running to lay down for the acceleration or deceleration. Nothing he could do during it.

And then he realized the advantage of it. He could lie on his cot and not have to do anything. He couldn't do anything so there was no guilt attached to it. It was an opportunity to do nothing other than relax.

This time there was no one in his cabin with him. Montgomery's body had been removed, and Davies was somewhere else. He realized that he kind of missed having her there. It made for an interesting couple of hours.

He turned his head slightly and looked at the screen of his computer. With the deceleration initiated, he had thought that the stars would begin to look like stars, but they hadn't. They hadn't slowed enough.

So Jefferson lay there and let his mind roam. Let his mind go from topic to topic without worrying about forcing it into channels. He didn't worry what they would do when they got to the planet's surface. He didn't worry about the logistics of getting them down there.

Instead he thought about Sergeant Mason. He realized that the sergeant hadn't been in his thoughts much lately. He knew that he owed everything to Mason. If the sergeant hadn't crawled out into the driving rain and the whithering fire from the enemy machine guns, Jefferson would never have won his medal and wouldn't be a colonel. Instead he'd probably be a first lieutenant somewhere, working under a major who'd never seen combat.

Mason had taught Jefferson so much. Mason had taught him that men weren't necessarily brave or cowards. Men did what they were trained to do, and if the training had been good enough, there was no time for fear or cowardice. A soldier did what he was trained to do.

Circumstances dictated who won medals and who didn't. Circumstances had gotten Jefferson the Galactic Silver Star. Mason should have gotten it, but Mason had gotten killed, so the brass had given him the medal. The generals preferred a live hero to a dead one.

Circumstances. That had done it.

Jefferson hadn't deserved the medal or the promotions. He hadn't understood the responsibilities of command. He hadn't understood that pinning eagles on a man's shoulders did not make him a colonel. It made him a kid with a lot of rank.

But now Jefferson felt he deserved the eagles. He had grown into them, and even if he hadn't deserved the medal, he'd been given it. He'd spent the last few years trying to prove that he was worthy of wearing it.

And now he was going to have the chance again. If the enemy attacked, there would be plenty of opportunities to prove that he was a brave man and deserved his medal. A single act made neither a hero nor a coward. A single act was merely a stage in the growth of the individual.

Once he'd understood that, he had felt better about the medal and his eagles. He'd found himself more tolerant of his subordinates. He'd found that he understood them better. He was becoming a good commanding officer, and he was learning how to be a real leader. Not a manager but a leader.

Jefferson fell asleep then. The pressure against him, the weight that seemed to be sitting on his chest was no longer important. Jefferson was relaxed and happy. It was the first time in months that he'd actively tried to relax.

* * *

There was an insistent bong on his computer. Without thinking about it, Jefferson rolled over and looked at the screen. As he did, he realized that the pressure of the deceleration was gone. They had slowed to sublight speed.

He got up and walked to the computer. "What?"

"Courier is in now. Ready for his debriefing."

"I'll be right there," said Jefferson. He looked at the tiny alcove that held his shower and wished for the time to take one. It would make him feel so much better, and as the colonel, they'd have to wait for him. That was a privilege of rank. But then it wasn't right to keep the troops waiting for him while he took the luxury of a shower.

Jefferson shut off the computer and left his cabin. He reached the mid-lift and then headed for the conference room. He walked the corridors where his soldiers and those of Colonel Davies were congregating. They all looked a little worse for wear. It had been a rough twenty-four hours but now it was over. Now they were about to planetfall and that would change the rules.

He entered the conference room and found Clemens with the courier, Torrence, Davies, and a couple members of her staff. Jefferson walked to the head of the table, glanced at the windows that showed normal space outside and then back at the assembled officers.

To the courier, he said, "You are?"

"Carson. I'm a scout for the division. They call me Kit."

"Fine," said Jefferson, sounding tired. "What have you got for me?"

Carson looked at Clemens who said, "He brought a computer disk. I've had it uploaded into our equipment. The information is a little ragged but understandable."

"You've reviewed it?" asked Jefferson.

"Yes, sir. While we were in deceleration. I wanted to have it ready for you."

Jefferson nodded, not sure that he liked having someone else reading his mail, although Clemens had a right to know the contents of material the courier brought. He decided not to say anything about it.

There was a moment's pause and then the computer began to speak, relaying the information. As it started, Clemens raised his voice to say, "This is the encapsuled version. If you want the whole thing, we can play it later." He hesitated and then added, "This will tell you about the Eighth."

"Report from Delaney," the computer said, "under attack in the Alpha Mensae system. Enemy is broadcasting a surrender demand using the languages of Earth. The implication is that they know who they face and that they know where the Earth is. Ultimate destination has to be the Earth."

Clemens said, "I'm not happy with that deduction. Just because the enemy broadcast all his surrender demands in Earth languages does not mean he is aware of Earth."

Jefferson waved him to silence as the computer continued. "We are now being bombarded. Concussion weapons with little shrapnel, designed to reduce our defenses. No evidence of either biological or chemical weapons being deployed. No nuclear weapons. Apparently they don't want to ruin the environment. That implies an occupying force."

"Not necessarily," said Clemens. "Might mean that their biological or chemical weapons won't work against us. Or are untested."

"Or they have none," said Carter.

Now Carson spoke, "From what I saw, they were occupying the planet. Delaney's assessment might have been correct."

The computer continued, "Landing forces are coming down in disc-shaped craft that might hold as many as fifty or sixty individuals. They're assembling a klick from our location, though I don't know why."

There was a hesitation and then, "Our weapons are effective against them but not as effective as I would have hoped. . . ."

Jefferson interrupted. "Then they've developed some defenses against our lasers. That makes sense."

Clemens ended the tape. "Not a lot of new information there. You can listen to the whole thing later."

Jefferson nodded. "Okay. That gives us some feel for what we're going to face. Conventional weapons. Standard attempt to reduce the defenses through cannonade and bombardment. I would assume a frontal assault of some kind." He looked at

Clemens. "You and the rest of the fleet can help us by not allowing them superiority in space."

"I would assume that the captain of Delaney's fleet would have tried the same thing."

"But you've faced them before," said Jefferson. "You know what to expect."

"True."

"Not to mention the upgraded weapons that were given to you," said Jefferson.

"Also true."

"The secret here," said Jefferson, "is to hit them with what they don't expect. We'll take all our weapons to the planet's surface and prepare to fight in a wide range of chemical or biological environments. We'll prepare to fight in a wide range of ways. Captain Clemens, once we're deployed, I might suggest that you go on the offensive. Don't wait for them to come to you. Go get them."

Clemens shrugged. "I'm not sure that'll do much good if their fleet is much larger than mine. Besides, we're not designed to wage a protracted war in space."

"The best defense is a good offense," said Jefferson.

"Don't quote time-worn clichés to me," said Clemens. "I know them all."

Jefferson turned his attention to Carson. "Anything else that you can tell us?"

"No, sir," said Carson. "I wasn't even aware of what was on the computer disc I was carrying."

"You didn't access it?"

"No, sir." Carson grinned. "I had other things to listen to. Besides, the mailman isn't supposed to read the mail. Just deliver it."

"I would have accessed it," said Torrence.

"Yes, ma'am," said Carson.

"Any comments on the deployment?" asked Jefferson.

"I think we'd better deploy closer together," said Davies. "That way we'd be in a better position to support one another."

"Of course, if we're separated by the planet, they'll either have to significantly divide their forces or ignore one of us. With floaters, we should be able to support one another."

"If we had a third regiment," said Davies.

Jefferson knew what she was thinking. Two of them would always be in a position to support one another, and the third would be a reserve force. Three regiments would make life easier. But they didn't have three, and although they could create a third by bleeding some of their strength, Jefferson couldn't see the advantages outweighing the disadvantages.

"We'll deploy so that we'll be in a better position to support one another," said Jefferson. He looked at Clemens. "How long until we achieve orbit?"

"Call it an hour at the outside."

Jefferson looked at Davies and then Torrence. "I want to begin planetfall in five hours, max. Carter, you'll provide the most suitable locations in the next two hours, based on the readings taken by Captain Clemens's staff. Questions? None? Then let's get at it."

Jefferson watched as the staff officers climbed to their feet. No one said a word. They knew what had to be done so that both regiments could deploy. He was momentarily surprised, thinking that the deployment was coming too quickly, but then realized that it was the reason that they'd gone through the uncomfortable routine of acceleration and deceleration. So that they would be in a position to deploy.

Torrence had stopped at the hatch. "Coming, Colonel?" she asked.

"Right behind you," he answered.

11

FLAGSHIP OF THE TENTH INTERPLANETARY INFANTRY REGIMENT

THEY'D MAKE PLANETFALL in the shuttles. No reason not to use them. It wasn't as if they were trying to sneak in. There was a solid-looking plain that wasn't far from where Jefferson wanted to establish his camp. The shuttles were designed to land on unimproved areas.

Torrence stood close to him in the control room off the shuttle bay and said, "Timetable calls for three days to get both regiments and all our gear on the ground. That's without pushing it."

Jefferson nodded. "At the moment there is no need to push it."

"I've ordered the First Battalion in first, then the engineers with their construction equipment, and then we'll deploy some of Davies's people, then back to ours, all based on the fleet's orbit. That's coordinated through Clemens and with Davies."

"Good."

She hesitated for a moment and then asked, "What do you think of Colonel Davies?"

"It's not politic for one commander to talk about another in front of subordinates."

Torrence nodded but grinned. "Except, as your second in

command, if anything happened to you, command would fall to me. I have to know."

"She's a capable officer," said Jefferson. He glanced at the technicians in the control room. They were busy with their own tasks and didn't have time to listen. He lowered his voice anyway. "She's a little unimaginative sometimes, but a capable officer."

"That's it?"

"What more do you want?"

Torrence rubbed a hand through her hair. "The two of you went through the acceleration together." She shrugged as if unsure of what she was asking.

"That was her doing, thinking that we could discuss the deployment of the regiments. She got to my cabin with only a minute or so to spare. There was nothing I could do."

"That explains it."

Again Jefferson checked the technicians. "You have something more on your mind?"

"Rumors from the troops," said Torrence. "There's been talk that the two of you were . . . more chummy than your positions dictated."

"I love it," said Jefferson. "Troops don't have enough to worry about. Now they've got to worry about what I do in my spare time."

"Troops don't like to think that you've got any spare time," said Torrence. "And they don't like it when their commander starts fraternizing with another commander."

"Well, they'll just have to worry about it then. But now, with the deployment coming, they'll have other things to do. They can concentrate on their jobs."

"Yes, sir. Do they have anything to worry about?"

Jefferson suddenly understood the question. He laughed out loud. Torrence was a good executive officer and she was a good friend. More than that, he decided. She was much more than a good friend. She wasn't worried about what the troops had to say. She wondered what her role was going to be.

"No," said Jefferson. "I'm concentrating on my own regiment. They'll just have to understand that since we're working together, I have command, in essence, of a light brigade, but my attentions will be focused on our regiment."

"Which doesn't answer the question," said Torrence.

Jefferson had to smile. "Then no. There is nothing to worry about."

"Good," said Torrence.

"Anything happening here that I should know about?"

"No, sir," said Torrence. "Everything's in the computer. All commanders have their orders and all NCOs have been briefed. Unless something happens, we'll begin deployment soon."

"When is the headquarters party scheduled?"

"Whenever you'd like to go, Colonel."

"I want to get some of both regiments on the ground and then let Davies remain here and I'll go on down."

"Yes, sir."

Jefferson spent his time wandering the ship, checking with the troops. They weren't happy about a deployment because it meant living in conditions that were less than perfect, but then, with the crowding on the ship, any change was welcomed. They just wanted to get at it because they didn't know what would happen once they were down.

Jefferson returned to his office and thought about that. If he thought it through, he knew that this deployment would be no different from the last. They would do the same things. They would face the same dangers. But the troops didn't think things through. All they could see was that they were landing on a planet that no one had explored and that frightened them.

He punched up the holo of the planet and watched as it spun slowly above the conference room table. He rocked back and studied it. A green glowing ball. Nothing outstanding on the planet. Average.

He heard the announcement that told him that the First Battalion was away. He didn't move as the deployment of Davies's regiment began. He sat there, letting the planet spin, but did reach down to engage the computer.

After an hour, he decided it was time to get the staff to the planet's surface. Get the command structure set up and begin to push the engineers to get the defenses erected.

He walked to the mid-lift and took it to his cabin. He stripped off his fatigues and put on the battledress. A uniform of mesh that would absorb the energy of the enemy's weapons. It had been updated and improved so that it was more effective. It could take a larger charge. He carried the hood and the gloves with him.

He thought about returning to the conference room, but then sat down and used the intercom. "Staff officers are to report in combat dress to the shuttle bay."

He'd almost ordered them to the conference room but there was no reason for that. No reason to sit there and look at a photographic mock-up of a planet that they would be walking on in a few hours. No reason to go over, again, the material, the intelligence reports, and the data that the probes had supplied. It was time to forget that and get to the job.

He picked up his hood and slipped it over his head so that only his eyes showed. There was a slit for his mouth so that he could eat and drink without taking it off. He put on his pistol belt and plugged in the powerpack. Now a laser hit would be absorbed and the energy used to power his own weapon.

Jefferson started for the hatch and was suddenly depressed. He didn't want to leave the cabin. He wanted to remain on the ship where the environment was controlled, where the food was hot, the water cold, and there were old movies scheduled through the day for those who were off duty and could find a view screen. Not the most luxurious of places but a hell of a lot better than a planet where no human had set foot until the colonization office had landed a ship for exploration.

He took a look around the cabin, feeling that he was never going to see it again. It was a ridiculous feeling that was like the dreams men sometimes had about their deaths in combat. He'd heard more than one story of a soldier who'd dreamed his death, or felt it coming, the cold breath of eternity on his neck, and who'd gone out and died. Jefferson had wondered if it had been a self-fulfilling prophesy. A man, or woman, believed that death was coming and then died.

But the feeling was so real. It was as real as a knife in the back. He was not going to see the cabin again. He shuttered, icy fingers grabbing at his stomach and massaging it. He turned suddenly, slammed a hand against the button at the side of the hatch and locked the cabin. He wanted to run, to fill his mind, but he couldn't do that. He wished there was someone around to talk to, something for him to do as he hurried to the mid-lift.

And then, as he entered, the feeling passed. He looked at the changing numbers and came to the shuttle bay deck. He exited the lift and saw the lines of soldiers ready for deployment.

Second Battalion was there. A large group he recognized. Men and women he'd talked to. He shouted, "Everyone ready to land?"

"Hell, no, Colonel," came a voice. "I'd rather stay right here and sleep."

"Nope," said Jefferson sounding artifically jovial. "We've got to go out and make the galaxy safe for the human race."

"Fuck 'em," yelled someone, and those in earshot burst into laughter.

"Wish we could," said Jefferson.

With the thoughts that had frightened him in his cabin forgotten, he hurried toward the main hatch. The light over it glowed bright green telling him it was safe to enter.

Inside, he could see one of the shuttles standing in front of him like a giant Easter egg, except the color was jet black so that it would make it difficult to see in space. It squatted on short legs that could be extended to compensate for uneven terrain on the planet's surface. Near the top was the hatch for the cockpit crew and a band of thick glass so that they could see to maneuver.

A sailor ran across the deck, slid to a stop and saluted. "Are you going to deploy now, Colonel?"

"As soon as we can get the staff down here, yes, we're going to deploy."

"That'll mess us up a little," said the sailor looking at the screen of his handheld computer.

"Very much?" asked Jefferson.

"How many people?" he asked.

"Immediate combat staff minus the exec. No more than ten people."

"Oh, that'll be fine then. You can go in this shuttle,

Boarding is about ready to begin. You can board now if you'd like, sir."

"My staff and I'll board last."

"Aye aye, sir."

Jefferson glanced across the shuttle bay floor and saw Torrence standing in the control room. She lifted a hand to acknowledge that he was there but no more.

Two more officers joined him. Carter from intelligence and then Winston from personnel. Courtney Norris, the supply officer and the youngest officer on his staff, appeared then, ready for planetfall.

"No need of the supply officer," said Jefferson, looking at Norris.

"If the regiment goes, I go," she said.

Jefferson nodded grimly, thinking that her remarks could be interpreted in a couple of ways. But he knew what she meant and everyone, but everyone, was deploying on this one.

"That's fine, Lieutenant."

Another couple arrived including the operations officer and the communications officer. They stood in a small group near the hatch of the shuttle, watching as the flight crew walked around it making the last of the inspections before they were dropped into space.

The main hatch to the shuttle bay opened and the troops began to enter, moving like a line of army ants marching through the jungle. They headed for the ramp that lead up into the shuttle, and then disappeared inside. One right after another.

A sailor stood at the hatch counting them and making sure that the right people were getting on the shuttle. If it crashed, they'd want to know who had died. A shuttle crash rarely left enough to be identified.

Finally he held up his hand and turned toward Jefferson. "Your staff now, Colonel."

"Thank you."

Peyton, the operations officer, asked, "Should we all be getting on the same shuttle?"

"No reason not to. Your assistant is competent as is Major

Torrence. If we die, they'll be in a good position to take over. Let's just do it."

As Peyton headed up the ramp, Norris slipped closer to Jefferson. "What do you mean by that?"

"By what?"

"By saying that it'll mean nothing if we die?"

Jefferson looked down at her. A pretty woman and a competent officer. She had a soft streak in her that would kill her in combat if she let it. That was one of the reasons she had been assigned to supply. The supply officer was rarely involved in combat.

"I don't believe that is what I said."

"Close enough."

"I simply meant the regiment would live on without us. A regiment has a life that transcends its members. The Seventh US Calvary didn't die with Custer at the Little Bighorn but fought on in Vietnam. The Twenty-fourth Regiment of Foot didn't die at Isandhlwana but lived on to fight at Rouke's Drift. I think that's all I meant."

"Not a very comforting thought," said Norris.

"Let's just get on board," said Jefferson.

"Yes, sir."

He followed her up the ramp but stopped at the top to look a final time at Torrence in the control room. As he stood there, he realized that his thoughts had again taken a morbid turn. A far too morbid turn.

He entered the shuttle, looked at the seats filled with the soldiers that were going to count on him and wondered if he'd be up to the task. If he'd be able to save them in the coming fight. Sergeant Mason would have told him to do his best, that no one could ask for more than that, but Sergeant Mason was dead. Sergeant Mason had done the best he could for his young lieutenant and had died doing it.

Jefferson felt the fear wash over him again. A crippling fear, unlike anything he'd felt since those terror-filled minutes in a driving rain while the pillbox raked the ground with its machine-gun fire.

In those few minutes he knew that he'd never see the ship again. This was the last time he would ever be on it. It was the last time he'd have anything to do with the ship and the people on it.

The feeling was so real, so intense, that it scared him badly.

"You okay, Colonel?" asked Norris. She hadn't moved to her seat yet.

Jefferson felt the blood drain from his face, felt the sweat bead and drip and wished that he could just lay down for a moment. He wished that he could get away from there, if only for a few minutes. To her, he said, "I'm fine. Just fine."

"Yes, sir," she said, not believing him.

"Take your seat, Lieutenant," he said. And then followed her into the shuttle. There was nothing else he could do.

12

ON THE PLANET OF EIGHTY-TWO ERIDANI

THE SHUTTLE STOOD in the center of a blackened expanse of forest, wisps of smoke rising from the destruction caused by the rocket engines as they landed. As soon as the hatch was opened, Jefferson was up and moving. He ran down it and out, across the ash-covered ground, his feet kicking up tiny clouds of the gray-black dust.

At the perimeter of the destruction, he threw himself down, his weapon ready. From the intelligence briefs, he knew that there was no intelligent creatures on the planet. There was nothing for him to worry about, but he still followed the directives. He still followed procedure, just in case someone had made a mistake.

The other officers, and then the rest of the troops, followed suit. As soon as the shuttle was empty, the equipment removed, the engines fired. They used just enough thrust to lift them away from the soldiers. At five thousand feet, the main engines fired, and the shuttle roared upward into the sky, heading back to the fleet.

The instant it was gone, Jefferson was up and moving, walking around the tiny perimeter they had established. He looked into the thick forest, at trees more than two hundred feet tall, some of them draped with thick curtains of vegetation that looked like Spanish moss. From inside the forest came a single, piercing call.

"What in the hell was that?" asked Norris.

Jefferson turned and found her standing next to him. He couldn't see much of her face with the hood in place. Just her bright eyes.

"One of those dinosaurs that Carter warned us about, I would imagine."

"I hope we don't see one."

Jefferson chuckled. "As a kid, didn't you dream of finding a lost world filled with dinosaurs? Hell, I must have seen a hundred videos about that. Now we're here and we've found it."

"Except we're not on an expedition to find dinosaurs," said Norris.

Jefferson had to agree with that. He saw that the other officers and the NCOs were getting a patrol ready to move the hundred meters to the right where the first battalion should be digging in.

There was fluttering overhead, like the flapping of a thousand leathery wings. A shadow flashed over them, and Jefferson looked up at a bird that had to have a wing span of more than thirty feet.

"Jesus!" said Norris, ducking instinctively.

But the creature, with a long pointed beak and huge, clawed feet, didn't seem interested in them. It screamed once, wheeled around, and disappeared over the forest.

"Dinosaur is right," she said.

Jefferson nodded toward the head of the column that was formed at the edge of the forest. "Let's go."

As he and Norris joined the column, it moved forward, beyond the soldiers beginning to create a perimeter there and entered the forest. Jefferson could see that the plants all seemed to be oversized. Nothing small anywhere. The bushes had thick trunks with broad leaves. The ferns grew to huge sizes, crowding out other plants. The trees were gigantic, the bark thick, looking like huge ropes attached to the trunk.

But the colors were right. Everything was green, from a

light, yellowish green to a deep verdant green. There were sprinklings of color, from flowers that were also huge. One of them was as big as a soldier and looked as if it could completely cover a body. There was a strong, pungent odor from it.

There was a loud buzzing. They found a huge hill filled with insects. A few of them, as big as a fist, hung in the air over the nest, as if they were an air patrol guarding it. They seemed to watch the soldiers but didn't attack.

A few moments later, as they wormed their way around the largest of the trees, following a path that had been worn in the forest by the animals, they found the First Battalion. They had expanded the area burned by their shuttle, had dropped some of the trees and were scraping the ground, removing the last of the vegetation. There were two fires in the center of the perimeter. Robots dropped by the resupply shuttle were working at building the defenses, at cutting away the jungle and at burning the debris.

Jefferson followed his soldiers into the center of the perimeter where Major Julie Laneer stood. All that Jefferson could tell was that she was a short woman, a stocky woman, though that might have been the result of the uniform she wore and the equipment she carried.

"Making good progress," she said as Jefferson approached. She didn't salute following the tradition that had developed in combat environments on Earth.

"I can see that. I'll have the Second Battalion begin to construct the underground tunnel and a trench system so that we can link up."

"Yes, sir." She reached up to wipe her forehead, but the hood covered her face, making that impossible.

"Carry on, Major," he said.

She nodded and moved back toward the perimeter. She had work to do.

As did they all. Lots to do before nightfall and lots more to do before the enemy arrived.

The command post was created in an underground bunker hollowed out by the engineer robots. Walls were made of thick armor, created from elements in the soil and burned into place by the robots. It was deep enough and the walls were thick enough that a small thermonuclear device detonated on the surface would not be enough to destroy it.

The electromagnetic radiation created by the radio and electronic equipment was shielded, and the antenna array was concealed in the forest more than a klick from the command post. If the enemy destroyed the antennas, a second array and then a third could be brought into play. The last resort was a number of small antennas over the command post.

The interior was cool and comfortable. The robots had created a number of desks, chairs, and even a couch that was long enough to sleep on. There were some maps on the walls, showing the positions of the regiment, showing Davies's regiment, and a few of the major terrain features they had discovered. Clemens, with the fleet, had supplied a dozen large aerial photos as well.

Jefferson sat in one of the chairs, his feet up on another. His fingers were laced behind his head and he was staring up at the recessed lighting of the bunker, thinking that things weren't all that bad. The troops, for the most part, had comfortable quarters, even if those quarters were in bunkers. There were heavy weapons protecting them, most using an automated acquisition and tracking system, and there was no sign of the enemy. None whatsoever.

After a week on the planet's surface, with work from dawn to dusk, with the rush to get a camp established, it seemed that life had never been better. They'd even brought down a few video machines and there were nightly tapes in the mess bunker, the supply bunker and sometimes in the command post.

Patrols reported sightings of dinosaurs, the largest standing nearly fifty feet tall. It had been attacking a smaller beast. The soldiers had killed the bigger and let the smaller get away. They'd been proud of themselves.

Torrence entered the command post, coming down the stairs, opening the metal blast door, and then stopped. She held a cup of coffee in her hand but wasn't drinking from it.

"I've got the people set for a ten percent alert tonight. Automatic systems should detect the enemy long before we can see them."

Jefferson turned slightly so that he could look at her. She moved across the plastic floor and then sat down. She held up the coffee.

"This is the most amazing thing. Hot coffee." She grinned. "I don't like coffee. I just find it amazing that we've been on this planet for only days and we've got all the comforts of home."

Jefferson nodded. He understood what she was saying. In the past, an army moved into a hostile environment and it was a luxury to be able to bathe. There was food that was little more than wormy bread, hardtack that was as hard as rock and coffee that was mud. Now, they had moved two regiments, a light brigade, across light years of space, and they were holding nightly movies for those who were off duty. They had clean, dry quarters, hot meals and entertainment, and they had done it in less than a week.

"You're not going to drink it?" asked Jefferson, pointing at the coffee.

"Not really. You want it?"

Jefferson leaned forward. "Sure." He took the coffee and tasted it. Still hot. But that was no surprise. It was in a thermal cup that managed to keep the hot beverages hot and the cold ones cold.

"Thanks," he said.

"Nothing to it," she said. "I was just amazed that we had it. Should be using C-rations and drinking coffee boiled in steel helmets."

"Except we don't have steel helmets," said Jefferson. "And C-rations went out long ago."

"True." She reached up and pulled at her hood, taking it off. She shook out her hair, ran a hand through it, and then said, "Maybe we could do without the *full* uniform for a couple of days."

Jefferson shook his head. "I know there are people out there who think I'm being chickenshit by insisting on complete combat gear when outside the bunkers, but it's the right move.

Get the troops in the habit of putting it on and it becomes second nature. They don't have to think about it. Might save a few lives and it's not all that uncomfortable."

"I suppose," she said tiredly. She leaned back and closed her eyes.

Jefferson sipped the coffee. He watched her for a couple of moments. Finally he said, "What's the feeling among the troops?"

Without opening her eyes, she said, "Now that they're down, the base is constructed and we're working a normal twelve-hour day, they've relaxed."

"Good," he said. He thought about the rush to get to Eighty-two Eridani, a rush that he had created. It was true that they had the camp in and they were refining it, that they were getting the automatic defense weapons up, and that they were making improvements daily.

Now Torrence opened her eyes. "Couple more days and this is going to be a strong position. It's going to take a major force to push us off."

"Uh-huh," said Jefferson. He didn't tell her that a fixed defensive position's greatest disadvantage was that it couldn't be moved. It conceded nearly every advantage to the enemy. But it did make the enemy attack *them*.

Torrence looked at her watch. "I suppose I'd better take a stroll around the perimeter. Let the troops know that we're still here and interested."

"Give me a moment and I'll go with you. I want to take a look at the changes made today."

"Certainly."

Jefferson drained the coffee and set the cup down on the floor. He stood and walked over to a bank of radios. All were turned on and all were listening. Jefferson had dictated there would be no radio communications unless absolutely necessary. Communications with Davies's regiment was over shielded, buried cable. Very little electromagnetic radiation to detect.

"Nothing going on, Colonel," said the NCOIC. Sergeant David Cooke was an intelligent, competent soldier who wouldn't be much good in a hand-to-hand fight but who could, if necessary, create a working radio from junk.

"I want a solid radio watch all night."

"Understood, sir."

Jefferson nodded. "I know that I don't have to tell you that."

"Yes, sir."

Jefferson turned. Torrence was pulling her hood over her head. She touched the powerpack at her belt, checked the leads, and then the laser pistol in its holster.

"I'm ready," she said.

Jefferson did the same. Lead by example was one of the things he'd learned. If the soldiers had to wear their protective gear at all times, if they had to have a weapon with them at all times, then he would do the same.

He walked to the blast door and pulled on the handle. It swung open easily, on huge, well oiled hinges. As Torrence stepped through, Cooke shouted. "Colonel, message coming in from Captain Clemens."

Jefferson felt his stomach turn over. He was suddenly sick because he knew what the message would be. Jefferson ran toward the radios. "Turn it up."

"Yes, sir."

Then he heard Clemens's voice. A calm voice with just a hint of excitement in it. "I say again. We've detected a fleet coming at us. Enemy fleet will be here inside the next twelve hours."

Jefferson took the mike and said, "You are cleared to maneuver for the protection of the fleet."

"Roger that. We will head out to engage them. Good luck to you."

Jefferson nodded and knew that Clemens couldn't see it on the radio. "Good luck to you too," he said.

Torrence, standing at the blast door asked, "What's going on?"

"Enemy has arrived," said Jefferson.

"How soon until they're here?"

"Twelve hours minimum. Clemens is going to maneuver to intercept."

"They going to come here?"

Jefferson nodded. "No other reason to be here, other than to attack us. They'll be coming soon."

"Shit," she said.

"My feelings exactly."

13

FLAGSHIP OF THE TENTH INTERPLANETARY INFANTRY REGIMENT

THE APPROACHING ENEMY fleet was barely visible at full magnification on the view screen. Clemens sat in the captain's chair, leaning forward slightly, one elbow supported by the arm, his chin cupped in his hand. His whole attention was focused on the enemy as he tried to count their ships. The black of space masked the enemy's fleet, making it difficult to see much of anything.

"How many?" he asked.

"Sensor count makes it twenty-five in the forward element. An additional fifteen in the second."

"Forty," said Clemens. "Any indication of the number of warships?"

"No, sir. Electromagnetic readings are much higher in the first group, but that could be explained by their attempts to scan us."

"Full view of the system," said Clemens.

The flatscreen changed slowly, showing the system from the point of view of Clemens's ship. The central star was down in one corner, a planet, several million miles away was centered, and the enemy fleet, had it been visible, would have been in the far corner from the star. It gave Clemens a perspective on his options, where he could deploy his ships, and his avenues of retreat, if he needed them.

He sat back and rubbed a hand over the back of his neck slowly, thinking. He'd met this enemy once before. But that had been the second string, and he was about to meet the front-line troops. These would be the best they had.

There was time to think. He touched the arm of the chair and said, "Captain Morrow."

A moment later Morrow appeared on the flatscreen. To him, Clemens said, "Take the troop ships, supply ships, and head on out. We'll screen your path."

"Aye aye, sir."

Morrow's image faded and the system reappeared. "Give me the enemy fleet."

They were closer now, spreading out in a flat line, all of them pointed right at Clemens and his ships. He thought about the last time. Missiles, lasers and beams had driven the enemy off during that battle, several months earlier. But Clemens didn't think they'd engaged warships.

He touched the arm of his chair. "Let's close everything up," he said. "All crews to their battle stations. All energy to be diverted to weapons systems and all non-essential equipment to be shut down."

He let go of the button and rocked back. "Distance and time to max range?"

There was a hesitation. "We can engage them in twenty-two minutes, but that's at an extreme range. Probably of inflicting damage is remote."

For a moment he watched the enemy fleet. Their ships looked small and insignificant, but Clemens knew that as they approached, that impression would change. This was a dangerous enemy. Very dangerous.

Clemens was conscious of the activity on the bridge around him. Men and women moving about the equipment, doing their jobs. There was a quiet chirp of electronic gear, buzzes from it, snaps and pops. There was quiet whispering as the officers did their jobs. They were monitoring the progress of the enemy fleet, they were searching for the electromagnetic signatures of the enemy's weapons. They were doing all the work while

Clemens sat and watched. But when shooting started, Clemens would be the man on the hot seat.

"They're about inside laser range. Missiles can be launched at any time."

Clemens nodded, his eyes fixed to the flatscreen. He didn't want to use his weapons early. Let the enemy get in close before he began shooting at them.

Now the enemy was close enough for him to see well with the flatscreen at full magnification. Their ships were only about three hundred meters long and maybe fifty or seventy-five wide. The surfaces were smooth with no wings, fins or evidence of firing ports, cannons, or hatches.

Clemens wasn't sure what he wanted to do. He knew that the enemy was coming at him. They had ignored the outer planets. Their path had never wavered.

"Screens up."

"Screens up, aye," said the Officer of the Deck.

"Targeting," said Clemens. He kept his eyes on the enemy ships displayed on the flatscreen.

"Targeting, aye."

"Have you acquired the enemy formation?"

"Aye, sir. We've been watching them for the last thirty minutes. They've moved into our range now."

"Stand by," said Clemens.

"Targeting, aye."

Quickly Clemens counted. Forty enemy ships that he could see. In two waves. Assume that the ships in the rear are support vessels. Those ships would hold the infantry to land on the planet, food, water, and new equipment, replacement equipment. Those would be the vulnerable ships.

Clemens wiped a hand over his face and was surprised to find that he was sweating. The air conditioning on the bridge, which normally kept it cooler than he liked so that the electronic equipment would continue to function properly, seemed to have stopped working. Clemens knew that wasn't true. It just felt like it.

The key to the battle then, would be to avoid contact with the warships and attack the second element. If his experience was any key, the support ships would not be armored as heavily as the warships. The theory would be that the support vessels would not be the targets of direct attacks. Especially with a screen of warships in front.

"Targeting," said Clemens.

"Targeting, aye."

"Is the second element in range of missiles and lasers?"

"Aye, sir. Barely."

"Concentrate your fire on the second element," said Clemens, "but do not fire until I give the orders."

"Targeting, aye."

Now Clemens turned to the communications officer. "Get me Captain Dillard on the *Concord*."

The enemy ships vanished as Dillard appeared. She was a young woman who had demonstrated her ability for command as they had fought the last battle. She had short-cropped hair and big brown eyes and looked too innocent to be a tough military commander.

"Dillard here."

"I want you to take your cruiser and two of the destroyers and maneuver to the right. Get an angle on the second enemy fleet and open fire on them the moment you have them in range. We'll support from here."

"Aye, sir."

Clemens punched his button again and Dillard was gone. The enemy fleet was closer, heading straight at him. They had separated slightly, the fifteen ships of the second group falling farther behind.

"Let's get ready, boys and girls," said Clemens, trying to keep his voice light, trying to convey the confidence that he didn't feel.

"They're beginning to accelerate."

"Where's Dillard and her ships?"

"They've pulled away, Captain. They're maneuvering for position now."

"Captain, Targeting."

"Go ahead, Targeting."

"Enemy ships are now in range of all our weapons. Do we fire?"

"Negative," said Clemens. He could feel his heart hammering in his chest. This was the hardest part. He had to delay the firing until the time was right. The enemy ships were roaring down on him. Wait too long and he would be overwhelmed before he could do a thing about it.

"Captain," said McCullough, the man in Targeting. "They're getting close."

"Target the second wave and tell me when they are in range. Lasers and missiles."

"They're in range now."

Clemens looked at the people on the bridge. "Show me Dillard's position."

The flatscreen changed. Now he could see Dillard's fleet off to the right, maneuvering toward the enemy. She hadn't closed with them.

"Targeting," said Clemens, "I want a spread of missiles fired at the first rank of enemy ships. Full spread. Twenty missiles. No lasers."

"Targeting, aye."

"That's going to do nothing," said Clemens's executive officer, Ginny Madison.

"Diverts attention," said Clemens.

"Missiles away," said McCullough in Targeting.

They appeared low on the flatscreen as pinpoints of light arcing toward the enemy. There was no response from the enemy fleet.

Dillard's fleet was off to the right, low, speeding toward a firing position. It didn't seem that the enemy had spotted her maneuvering. Or maybe they didn't care.

Beams flashed suddenly from the enemy. Points of light stabbing into the blackness. One by one, the missiles detonated in flashes of brightness as they consumed themselves. In an instant, the missiles had been eliminated.

"That was easy for them," said Madison.

"Twenty missiles against forty ships," said Clemens. "Hell, you don't even need computers to deal with a threat like that. Kids could do it."

"Then why?"

"Covering fire," said Clemens.

As he spoke, Dillard opened up. Her cruiser and both the destroyers, firing at the second wave.

"Targeting," said Clemens. "You are cleared to fire on the second wave of ships. Only the second wave."

"Targeting, aye."

More missiles and now the lasers too. And the torpedoes. All launched at once and aimed at the supply ships of the second wave. Coupled with the attack by Dillard, Clemens expected the enemy to begin a withdrawal. A temporary one.

But as Dillard opened fire, the enemy fleet turned as one. It looked as if the sides of their ships had erupted in fire. All of it directed at Dillard's ships.

"We're taking some heavy firing. Screens holding," said Dillard.

"Targeting," said Clemens. "Give them another volley."

"Targeting, aye."

But the enemy was no longer concerned with Clemens and the main body of the fleet. They were attacking Dillard in mass. Firing missiles and lasers. Space was alive with the technicolor displays. Explosions from the missiles. The beams of the lasers and the superheating of Dillard's ships.

Dillard was fighting back, forgetting about the second wave. She was directing her weapons against the forty enemy ships turned against her.

Clemens stabbed at the button on the arm of his chair. "Targeting, hit the second wave. Everything. Now."

"Targeting, aye."

Clemens watched as the destroyer on Dillard's right flank began to glow a dull cherry red as the hull began to super heat. It flared a moment later, first a bright red and then a blasing yellow. The flash radiated out and a cloud of debris began to spread.

"Lost one," said Dillard. Her voice was calm as if she was explaining that the weather would grow cold.

"Roger. Withdraw," said Clemens.

But it was too late for that. The enemy pressed forward, firing at the remaining two ships.

"Targeting," said Clemens. "Hit them hard."

"Targeting, aye.

But the enemy didn't respond to the attack by Clemens. They fired at Dillard's remaining two ships. The second destroyer turned suddenly and dove away, spiraling down, as defined by the ecliptic plane.

Dillard salvoed everything she had. All the missiles, torpedoes and the laser weapons. She reversed course, fighting as she retreated.

One of the enemy ships in the second wave flared and vanished. A sudden explosion that destroyed it. As that happened, the remaining fourteen ships turned and began to move toward the outer limits of the system.

But the main enemy fleet continued to attack. Their weapons crushed the screens shielding Dillard's cruiser in a matter of seconds. The hull began to superheat and glowed a brilliant cherry.

The final message was broken and garbled. Dillard's image flashed, was suddenly bright and clear, and then faded on the flatscreen. Smoke curled around her image as her ship began to burn.

"We've failed . . . trying to . . . in the . . . been good to know you." Dillard faded.

"Lost contact," said the communications officer, quietly, one hand pressed against his ear.

Clemens nodded and didn't demand that contact be reestablished. He knew what it meant. On the flatscreen he could see the final moments of Dillard and her cruiser. It was glowing brightly and pieces were breaking off, spinning away. There was no final explosion that ripped it apart. Just a disintegration as the ship broke up, like a fragile tanker against rocks in heavy seas.

Clemens turned away from that. He touched the button of the chair. "Targeting, you may fire at will."

"Aye, sir."

"Helm, let's get the hell out of here."

"Aye, sir."

14

ON THE PLANET'S SURFACE

JEFFERSON HAD MOVED across the plastic floor of the command bunker to the communications gear. There was a single, small flatscreen mounted on the plastic wall. They could pick up signals from space, but the quality of those signals wasn't as good as those on the ship. Besides, he didn't want to create much in the way of electromagnetic radiation. The enemy could detect it and use it against him. Use it to guide his weapons.

Now, however, it was imperative that he witness the battle in space. He had to know what the enemy was doing and how Clemens was faring against them. The decisions he made in the next few hours could mean the difference between life and death for him and the regiment.

He stood to the side, the hood of his uniform held in one hand and his weapon in the other. He watched as the images on the flatscreen, little more than gray blobs on the black background, maneuvered. It was almost impossible to tell his fleet from the enemy. Almost.

As he watched, one of his ships vanished, then one of the enemy's, and then two more of his. Clemens, in the main body of the fleet, suddenly reversed course, and it looked as if Clemens was running from the fight.

"Hey," yelled the NCOIC, suddenly angry. "He can't do that—fucking coward."

"Clemens will do all right," said Jefferson automatically. "He won't leave us."

But the evidence on the screen seemed to say otherwise. It didn't look as if Clemens was going to stand and fight. Of course, in space it would be nearly impossible to run and hide. Too little cover for that.

Torrence, who stood just behind Jefferson, now wore her hood so that only her eyes and mouth were exposed. She held her weapon at port arms, as if ready to run from the command bunker. "Troops have to be alerted."

Jefferson turned and glanced at her. He nodded but said, "In a moment. We're going to have to shut down the major power sources anyway. Don't want them to show the enemy where we are."

"Enemy's got to know," said Torrence. "They moved on the fleet."

"That only means they know where the fleet is," said Jefferson. "We don't have to make them a present of our location just yet."

"Yes, sir."

"Full alert now. All crew-served weapons manned and ready. Computers up and running. No one sleeps, eats, or takes a piss until we know what's going to happen in the next few hours."

"Yes, sir."

Jefferson stood still for a moment, thinking. "I'm sure that Davies knows what's happening." He glanced back at the RTO. "You contact Colonel Davies and tell her that our fleet is under attack."

"Yes, sir." The RTO turned and touched the front of one of the radios.

Jefferson now concentrated on Torrence. He looked her in the eye but couldn't tell what she was thinking. The hood hid her facial expression. "You okay?" he asked.

"I'm fine. I'm not looking forward to this."

"Neither am I, but we've faced these guys before. We've beaten these guys before."

Torrence nodded but she knew, just as Jefferson did, that they had never faced the front-line troops. It had been more of a police force.

To Jefferson, she said, "I don't think they're looking for slaves this time."

"No," he said. And then he thought of the weapon, or the device, they'd used the first time. A beam that swept down and lifted people up. A teleportation device of some kind. The divisional science office had told him that they could screen against it, now that they knew it was there. A simple electromagnetic screen that inhibited, or interrupted, the signal and negated its potency. That's what he'd been told, but no one had ever tried it.

"Okay," he said, "let's get the screen turned on and then get the troops ready."

"Yes, sir." She turned to go, but then stopped, looking back at him. "Good luck. See you later."

"Good luck to you," said Jefferson. But he felt a growing fear in his stomach. The same fear he'd felt on the ship as they had made ready to deploy. A disaster was waiting for them. He was sure of it.

"Colonel," said one of the NCOs, "it's beginning to look real bad."

Jefferson turned. The fleet was accelerating, dropping toward Eighty-two Eridani. Jefferson knew that was to pick up speed. Use the gravitational pull of the star to accelerate in much the same way a car could use a hill. They'd then "sling-shot" out into space. And maybe the entire enemy fleet would go with them.

Jefferson hoped they would, but knew that they wouldn't. Clemens was outnumbered by better than two to one. The advantages all lay at the enemy's door. He had none.

"I've no signal from Captain Dillard," said the communications officer.

"Dillard is gone," said Clemens. "Helm, I want full power to the engines."

"Helm, aye."

"But . . ."

Clemens shot a glance at the communications officer. The woman seemed stunned, as if she couldn't comprehend what was happening now. As if her mind had suddenly shut down.

"Message to Jefferson," said Clemens. "Tell him that I am initiating Plan B."

"Plan B?"

"Yes." Clemens grinned briefly, remembering the old joke about there being no Plan B. But this time there was one. He had initiated it when he'd turned the fleet to flee the battle. Draw the enemy away from the planet's surface.

"Enemy ships coming at us," said one of the officers. "Closing rapidly now."

"Targeting, you have the enemy plotted?" asked Clemens.

"Targeting, aye, Captain. We are prepared."

"Scatter the sonic mines now. Full spread, spherical formation."

"Roger . . . mines deploying."

"Communications, get me Captain Boyson on the *Ohio*."

There was a pause and then Boyson appeared on the flatscreen. "Boyson here."

"Jake," said Clemens. "We're in deep shit here. You ready for the diversionary run?"

"Certainly. I don't know what good it will do, considering what happened to Dillard."

"You don't have to sacrifice yourself or your ship," said Clemens. "Just draw some attention away from us."

"Aye aye, sir." Boyson's image faded from the flatscreen.

"Radar Plot, Captain."

Clemens answered. "Go."

"Sir, their formation is beginning to fragment further. They've broken fifteen ships off to chase us, but the other ten are falling back toward their second line."

"Targeting," said Clemens.

"We monitored that, Captain."

"Distance to sonic mines?"

"They're approaching them now. No indication that they've seen them or detected them."

"*Ohio*, you are cleared to maneuver now," said Clemens.

"*Ohio*, aye."

"Communications, put it on the flatscreen. And I want the minefield shown."

The images on the flatscreen changed slowly, dissolving from one picture to the next. The enemy ships were now in the top left corner, easily visible. The minefield was between the two forces, invisible to the naked eye. Boyson's ship was a small spot down on the lower left, maneuvering for position. It flashed as it launched a spread of missiles and then seemed to dive away from the enemy.

Two of the enemy ships turned to meet the new threat. They sparkled as they fired their lasers and beams, targeting the missiles coming at them. As they did, Boyson fired again, more missiles and a number of torpedoes. These rocketed ahead of the missiles, corkscrewing toward the enemy ships.

And then the main force was in the sonic minefield. The lead ship flared and disappeared. A second flashed and broke apart, the two ends spinning away from a fiery cloud of spreading debris.

Suddenly the enemy reversed course, but that didn't help. More of the mines detonated. Another ship disappeared. And then a forth. Another began to glow, looking as if the rear was on fire.

"Targeting," said Clemens. "Let's hit them."

"Targeting, aye."

"Helm, reverse course."

"Helm, aye."

Clemens rocked back in his command chair. He watched the flatscreen as the enemy ships worked to retreat from the minefield.

"Targeting, detonate them all now," ordered Clemens.

"Targeting, aye.

The center of the screen flared into a brightness that washed out everything on it. The glow faded slowly, and it was obvious that a number of enemy ships had been damaged in the explosions.

But then they were clear of the mines and they turned to fight. Missiles, torpedoes and lasers flashed. Clemens saw the enemy fleet erupt again.

"Targeting, you are cleared to fire. Individual missiles coming in."

"Targeting, aye."

"Communications, tell the fleet to maneuver for its safety. All ships are cleared to fire."

"Communications, aye."

Clemens took a deep breath and studied the flatscreen. The missiles racing toward them. One of them flared and vanished. A second was hit, tumbled off, flames shooting from its sides. It hit a second and both of them exploded.

Another barrage of missiles was launched following the first. Two or three hundred of them bearing down on Clemens but ignoring the rest of the fleet.

"Helm, we need full speed, one hundred and eighty degrees. Now."

"Helm, roger."

"Targeting . . ." said Clemens. He pushed himself back in his chair, as if that could save him. He felt his arms and legs tense.

"Targeting, aye. We're working. Computers are . . . Wait one."

"Communications," said Clemens. "Have everyone target the incoming missiles."

Beams flashed from the other ships in the fleet. The front rank of missiles was hit with a solid wave of laser and beam fire and all detonated. There was a single, bright flash that consumed the missiles.

But behind that were more missiles. Clemens watched as the lasers fired, touching a few of them. But the remainder took evasive action, diving and climbing, dodging right and left.

Now the enemy fired their lasers and their particle beams. One of them brushed Clemens's ship and then slid away. Another hit but did nothing yet.

"Shields are taking a beating, Captain."

Clemens nodded but said nothing. He was more concerned about the missiles. They could rip his ship apart in seconds. They had to get them before he could worry about anything else.

And then one of his ships dove on the enemy formation,

firing at it. A ship exploded in a violent flash of light. Missiles, launched by the attacker, hammered into three others. One of them was gone in a flash but the other two seemed to dive out of the explosions, firing back at the aggressor with missiles and lasers.

"Targeting," said Clemens. "Two ships have broken formation."

"We've got them."

"Hit them."

"Targeting, aye."

"Helm," said Clemens, his voice tight with excitement. He kept his eyes on the flatscreen.

"I'm doing everything I can, Captain," said the Helmsman. "We're approaching full speed."

More of the enemy missiles flared and vanished, but there were always more of them behind those destroyed. Now the enemy fleet was beginning to advance on him again. They were chasing him toward the star. Clemens wondered if they had a plan that used the gravitational pull of the star, but couldn't see how they could make it work.

"Captain," yelled the plot officer, "missiles are falling away. They're out of fuel."

Clemens knew that they would not be accelerating unless they began to fall into the star. As he moved off to the right or left, the missiles would miss by a wider margin. The missiles no longer controlled the fight.

"Targeting, you are cleared to fire on the enemy fleet," said Clemens.

"Targeting, aye."

"Communications, rally the fleet to me. Recall everyone except the support vessels."

"Communications, aye."

Clemens relaxed slightly. The complexion of the fight was changing. Enemy ships had been destroyed. Many of them. But he was still badly outnumbered. The only positive thing that could be said was that he'd prevented the enemy from landing on the planet. Jefferson, Davies, and their regiments already on the ground were safe.

For the moment.

15

ON THE PLANET'S SURFACE

CLEMENS HAD THOUGHT that the regiments on the planet's surface were safe for the moment, but he had been wrong. With the majority of his fleet engaged in the running fight, a few of the enemy's ships in the second wave had broken away. They had dropped down, diving away from the fighting, and then had turned directly toward the planet that held the infantry.

Jefferson, watching the fight on his flatscreen, hadn't seen the maneuver. The capability of his instruments didn't allow much discrimination at the longest ranges. He saw them vanish, but then the curve of the horizon blocked his view. He didn't think anything about it.

"Colonel, we've got somebody coming in," said one of the NCOs.

Torrence moved forward and studied the screen. She turned toward Jefferson. "Looks like two enemy warships."

Jefferson nodded as if uninterested and then said, "Bombing attack." His voice rose. "Have the regiment stand by for a bombing attack!"

"Yes, sir." Torrence whirled and ran up the steps toward the blast door.

Jefferson stood his ground for a moment, looking at the

flatscreen. He watched as the last of his fleet vanished, out of range of his instruments. He hoped that Clemens and the majority of the fleet had survived, but at the moment he didn't have the time to worry about it.

To the NCOIC, Jefferson said, "You keep a close watch on that. Anything happens, you let me know."

"Yes, sir."

Jefferson then left the bunker. He opened the blast door and was hit by the heat and humidity of the planet. Sweat beaded immediately and dripped. It wasn't the kind of environment Jefferson liked.

He stopped long enough to pull the hood down over his head, making it even worse. Hot and humid, and now he was wearing a hood that tended to trap the heat. The hood did not "breathe" well.

The perimeter was in good shape. The bunkers, sunk into the soft ground, had been dug by robots, then lined with plastics designed to absorb shrapnel and overlayed with a mesh like that of the uniforms. It would redirect laser and beam energy into powerpacks.

There were few people moving above ground. Two soldiers ran toward a corner bunker. Another headed for a pulse laser that was on standby. It would fire at incoming enemy ships, if those ships approached too close and too fast.

There was a quiet whistling overhead, and Jefferson looked up in time to see a single flash. The enemy had arrived. They were beginning the attack.

Without waiting, one of the pulse laser batteries swung around and began to fire. Bright bursts of light flared up at a target he could not see. There was a brilliant flash and moments later a deep rumbling that reminded Jefferson of a thunderstorm on Earth. The laser was targeting the bombs, destroying them before they could reach the ground.

A warning siren went off and then the attack began for real. Jefferson could see the enemy ships, two of them, weaving in and out of the clouds. The bombs began to fall, and laser beams began to dance over the compound, superheating the ground and creating great hissing clouds of steam.

The defensive weapons began to shoot. Beams flashing up,

at the enemy ships that were corkscrewing through the air, dodging the beams as they dropped more of the bombs.

Jefferson stood flatfooted from a moment, watching the attack. He didn't believe that the bombs or lasers would hit him. Not that quickly. He watched as explosions mushroomed in the jungle to the west, the line of detonations coming at him in much the same way that mortars were walked to their targets.

Finally he turned and ran back toward the command bunker. He hit the blast door, shoved, and then fell into the bunker as the interior of the compound erupted into smoke and flame. He could hear shrapnel rattling against the bunker and smell the acrid stench of the burned explosives.

"Status report," he yelled.

"Weapons firing at enemy ships. Targeting the bombs and rockets being fired. No evidence of damage to our facilities and no casualties at the moment."

"Davies?"

"We've no contact with her at the moment. I think our shielded cable was destroyed."

Jefferson wanted to wipe his face, but the hood covered it. He stared at the radios and communications gear and wondered if he should alert Davies. She would have to know that he was under attack. They were probably hitting her camp as well.

"Keep monitoring," said Jefferson.

"Yes, sir."

Jefferson turned and ran back to the blast door, but didn't exit. He could hear the rumbling outside as the bombs detonated. He could feel the concussions through the floor. He shot a glance back at the communications technicians, but they sat calmly in front of their equipment, watching and listening.

The NCOIC raised his voice. "Lasers report they've damaged one enemy vessel. More coming in."

Jefferson stood up. "How many?"

"Ten or twelve. This could be it,sir."

"Alert the troops. Ground attack might be imminent and keep the defensive batteries firing."

"Yes, sir."

Jefferson could stand it no longer. He should stay in the

command bunker, but he wanted to see the damage outside. Not viewed on a flatscreen that could hide the subtleties of the damage. But see it for himself.

He moved against the blast door and made his way to the surface. Smoke hung heavy in the air. A few fires burned, consuming the debris created in the bombing. In the distance smoke rose, looking as if one of the enemy vessels had crashed into the trees.

There were people up and moving. One wore a red cross on the back of her uniform. That was a medic, running toward a bunker that looked as if it had collapsed. Others were crawling over it, digging. Jefferson didn't like that. Too many people exposed in one place.

Torrence appeared out of nowhere and said, "We've lost one laser battery. Four killed. And one bunker. We're checking now."

"Spread those people out."

"Yes, sir."

"The attack will come in a moment," said Jefferson. "We've got to be ready for it."

"Yes, sir."

He stood there, looking at the smoke from the wreck of the enemy ship and thinking that war had not changed since the first humans attacked one another. With all the sophisticated technology that could be brought to bear, it was still the foot soldier, the infantry, who determined the final outcome. People could roam space, but now the fighting was going to come down to what he could do on the planet's surface against another enemy who wanted to take the ground away from him.

The bombing did almost no damage to Davies's position. Everything was buried too deep and was too heavily armored for the enemy to succeed. She stood in her command post, watched the bombing on the flatscreen and found herself grinning. The enemy was coming, the enemy was attacking, but it was doing no good.

"Communications with Jefferson?" she asked.

"Out."

"Then we must assume that he is under attack as well. Let's prepare to meet the enemy."

"Yes, ma'am."

Forgetting her hood, she ran up the stairs and out of the command bunker. Damage to her position was minimal. There were craters in the center of it, some of them smoking, but the bunkers and the laser battery positions were all intact. The only real damage was the destruction of the shielded cable that ran to Jefferson's regiment.

Her troops were beginning to stumble out into the open, like the survivors of a tornado coming out of their storm cellars to see the destruction. But those were civilians, and soldiers should know better.

"Back to your positions," ordered Davies.

One or two of them looked at her, but they began to straggle back into their bunkers. A sergeant ran up to her, didn't salute, and said, "We've got something happening on the eastern perimeter."

"Come with me," she said and then spun, running back into the command bunker.

Once there, she studied the flatscreen and then ordered. "Give me the eastern perimeter."

"Yes, ma'am."

The view on the flatscreen changed radically. Now, at the edge of the jungle, at the edge of the plain they had cleared as a kill zone, she could see the beginnings of the enemy assault.

Davies took a step forward to see better. The enemy soldiers were lining up just as the British soldiers had once done before an assault on a fortified position. A primitive way to fight a war, when there were better ways, especially when the enemy had complete air and space superiority.

Davies turned and looked at one of the NCOs. To herself, she said, "Clemens must still be fighting."

The enemy began a slow advance across the open ground. Firing erupted from their ships covering the assault. They targeted the pulse lasers and beam weapons. Flashes of light hit the bunkers and was absorbed.

"Open fire immediately. Rake their assault force."

Now the pulse lasers fired, but the beams were absorbed by

something. The beams seemed to hit an obstacle and then vanished. They did not hit the enemy soldiers who were advancing under an umbrella shield of some kind.

Firing from the soldiers erupted. The lasers shot out and were absorbed by the screen. It began to glow, shimmering like the heat off sand on a hot summer day.

Someone opened fire with an old rifle. The slugs penetrated the screen easily. The enemy began to fall. One or two and then half a dozen as the soldiers switched to full auto.

Others saw the results and tossed away the laser weapons, using the older rifles. Now they were beginning to tear holes in the enemy lines.

"They're not geared to fight with primitive weapons." Davies moved forward and hit a button on one of the radio consoles. "Everyone switch to twentieth century weapons."

Now they were using grenade launchers. There were small explosions among the enemy soldiers, but still they came on, ignoring those dying around them.

The enemy's support continued to pour fire into Davies's regiment. Laser batteries shot back, but the outer covers began to glow. They could not dissipate the energy fast enough. The enemy's weapons were too strong. The crew from one abandoned it, running from it as it exploded. The force of the detonation slammed the crew to the ground. Only one of them got up.

The enemy's lasers raked the ground in front of the bunkers, creating clouds of steam. They hammered at the positions, the energy being absorbed, but then the enemy learned what to do. They concentrated on a single target. All lasers firing at it at once. In seconds the grid system fused and the energy ripped the lasers and beam weapons apart.

But the hammering of the old weapons kept tearing holes in the enemy's formation. Mortar crews began to target the enemy's support weapons, walking the mortar rounds into the lasers and particle beams.

They hit one of them. The explosion was obvious. The smoke began to pour from it and the crew ran from it. Then, just as had happened when the laser battery had been destroyed, the enemy installation blew up. There was a flash of bright light and then a loud, flat bang. The concussion hit Davies's bunkerline. It knocked some of the enemy from their feet.

"Get in touch with Jefferson," said Davies. "Tell him that the lasers aren't any good but the old rifles are. Break the radio silence."

"That'll give them our position."

Davies turned and stared at the communications NCO as if he'd suddenly grown a third eye. "Are you stupid? Don't you think they know where we are? Just send the Goddamned message."

"Yes, ma'am."

"Give me a scan of the whole perimeter."

The scene on the flatscreen changed. It looked as if someone were standing on a high point, spinning the camera slowly so that Davies could see the entire perimeter. The enemy was massing its assault, attacking at only a single point.

The problem was that the enemy was not being stopped. Their growing number of casualties didn't bother them. They came on under the protective umbrella of the anti-energy screen.

Even in the bunker, she could hear the hammering of the automatic weapons. It sounded like an old War Two movie. American Marines attacking Japanese strongholds.

"I'll be topside," she said. "You get anything in here, you make sure that I'm kept advised."

"Yes, ma'am."

Davies headed back up. As she pushed the blast door open, she was stunned by the difference. Smoke filled the air. The hammering of weapons was a din that was louder than anything she had experienced. The air was electric with the passing of the enemy beams. The hair on the back of her head stood on end, and she was suddenly apprehensive.

She slipped to one knee. Over the tops of the bunkers, she could see the enemy soldiers, coming on with the relentlessness of the tides. Small, gray creatures, firing their laser and energy weapons.

Now they were only a few feet from the perimeter. The firing was more intense. Few lasers and hundreds of rifles. The ground around the enemy churned as the bullets struck it. Tracers, looking almost like the beams of the lasers, flashed, hit, and then tumbled. A hundred of the little gray men were hit and fell, but there were always more of them. It was as if they were springing from the ground. Always more behind those who were shot and killed.

Davies, ducking low, ran along the side of the command bunker, heading for a position on the line. She dropped to the ground, crawling forward, the lasers slicing through the air over her head.

She slipped into the rear of the bunker. The firing of the rifles bounced off the walls. The interior was hot from the firing. Hot brass bounced on the floor as the men and women worked to stop the enemy attack.

Moving forward to the firing port, she could see the enemy swarming across the open plain. Nothing was going to stop them. Dozens fell, cut down by the automatic weapons' fire but that made no difference. More of them came on.

Davies leaned forward, her laser weapon aimed out. She fired and watched as the beam was absorbed by the invisible umbrella over the enemy formation.

But even with everyone firing old-fashioned weapons, cutting down the enemy soldiers, they reached the perimeter. They fired into the bunkers, their beams penetrating the firing ports. They crouched in front of them, shooting at the soldiers inside. The uniforms absorbed the first of the enemy, but there was too much of it. Powerpacks began to howl as the overloads burned out the systems.

The men and women rushed from the bunkers, trying to get away from those with the malfunctioning powerpacks. There were dull explosions as the packs detonated. Those close were killed by the concussions or the shrapnel.

But now everyone was outside, above ground, with the enemy pushing into the perimeter. The fighting was quickly hand to hand. The tall humans, towering a foot or more above the humanoid grays, punched, stabbed and clubbed the little creatures. But there were too many of them. For each one killed, two more appeared.

Davies backed away from the perimeter as her line began to

collapse. One of them ran at her and she instinctively fired from the hip. The laser beam touched the creature on the chest, held there for a moment and then burned through. They'd left the screen behind them. The creature fell forward, flat on the face, skidding.

In the din of the battle, she heard the screams of pain from her people. A dozen of them fell. A dozen more. And then there were bodies everywhere. A hundred of them. Two hundred. And more of the enemy coming on every second.

Davies turned to run. Not to escape but to reach the command bunker. She wanted to warn Jefferson. Had to warn him because there wasn't much more she could do.

She reached the blast door and grabbed it but it wouldn't swing open. The NCOs had locked themselves inside. She turned, saw the enemy coming at her, killing her regiment as quickly as they could. She hammered on the solid metal of the door, knowing that she could be shooting at it with a howitzer and they wouldn't hear her.

"*Open up!*" she ordered in frustration. She wanted to warn Jefferson. She owed him that much. She slammed a hand into the door and felt the bones break. There was a momentary shock of pain caused more by the sound of the breaking bones than from the actual damage.

She whirled and saw two of the grays coming at her. She fired again and hit the first in the top of the head. The laser beam sliced through the bone neatly, opening the skull so that she could see the gray-pink brain. The creature dropped to its hands and knees, flopped over and began kicking spasmotically as it died.

The second fired, but Davies's uniform absorbed the energy of its weapon. She turned slightly and then kicked up and out, catching the enemy on the side of the head. It spun away, hit the side of the command bunker and fell on its back. Davies leaped at it, jamming her knee into its chest. She punched at it, hitting it in the throat. It gagged once and turned its head away as blood poured from its mouth. She struck again, the force of the blow killing it.

Leaping to her feet, she backed away, her spine against the solid plastic of the bunker. Around her the regiment was dying rapidly. The firing, the screaming, had dropped off. Few of her people survived, though there were hundreds of enemy soldiers inside the perimeter.

A laser beam caught her on the cheek, pain flaring momentarily, turning her world white. As her vision cleared slowly, she saw the last of her people fall. She was alone in the perimeter except for the few survivors still fighting in the bunkers.

No chance to warn Jefferson. She hoped he would be able to do better. She had failed miserably.

And then the enemy turned on her, a dozen of them firing at once. There was only a moment to realize that she was not going to survive.

16

ON THE PLANET'S SURFACE

THE RADIO CONTACT that had been established with Davies's regiment was suddenly lost. Jefferson, who had walked back down into his own command post, heard the radio broadcast. There was no visual contact with Davies. Just the one radio link.

"They're under heavy attack," said the NCOIC, David Cooke.

Jefferson nodded. The flatscreen still showed the activities in space. Clemens's ships were disappearing quickly. It looked as if the enemy would be able to overrun the planet in a matter of hours. Jefferson had expected them to hold out for weeks, tying down enemy forces as they attempted to eliminate the Earth troops.

"Can you raise Colonel Davies?"

"I can try, sir."

Jefferson thought about it for a moment. If Davies was being attacked, the last thing she needed was a radio message from him. But then he needed intelligence that he couldn't get any other way. Not with Clemens trying to save himself in space. That had taken his space eyes away.

"Do it."

"We've got heavy activity coming from the east," said a technician. "Enemy ships."

"From the direction of Davies's camp?"

"Yes, sir."

"Shit," said Jefferson. "Okay. Let's prepare for an assault, and let's assume that Davies has been overrun."

"Colonel," said Cooke, "Davies reported that her lasers were not effective but that the old rifles, the slug throwers, were ripping the enemy to shreds."

"We already received that intelligence from the scout," said Jefferson. "You pass the word. I want the lasers targeted at crew-served weapons and enemy ships."

"Yes, sir."

Jefferson whirled and ran from the command post. He hesitated at the top of the stairs, standing there, looking at the smoking remains of his camp. The damage was light but it gave an indication of what the enemy could do.

Overhead the air was split by a roar. Jefferson looked up as the enemy ships shot over, heading toward the jungle at the far end of the kill zone. As they did, the pulse lasers and the particle beam weapons opened fire. Flashes of bright color reached up to scrape the undersides of the enemy's ships. The rear of one flared, as if it had suddenly burst into flame. It dived, climbed and then spiraled off, out of control like a balloon that was losing its air.

Jefferson watched the enemy land just outside of effective small-arms range. The ships were arranged in a semicircle, like a barricade to protect them. There was movement behind those ships as the enemy formed for the assault.

Torrence appeared, breathing hard. She took a swipe at her face, as if to wipe away the sweat, but the hood wouldn't allow it.

"Looks like they're going to come for real," she said.

"We ready?"

"As ready as we can be. The old rifles are distributed. Heavy machine guns are in place." She shrugged. "I can't believe this is the way to do it."

"We'll know in a few minutes," said Jefferson, "but all our intelligence suggests that it'll work."

A machine gun began to hammer, the tracers looping out over the open ground. They struck the ships, bouncing off them and tumbling away.

"Little early for that," said Torrence.

"We've got plenty of ammo. Let them know we're here."

The enemy responded, a laser flashing. The beams struck the bunker line and were absorbed easily. It was just a feeling-out as the two sides shot at one another.

Jefferson looked up into the sky. "Funny they don't have more in the way of support."

"Maybe Clemens is doing his job."

"Doing it well," said Jefferson. "We've got them split the way we want them."

It seemed that Torrence grinned, though it was nearly impossible to tell because of the hood. "We've got them where we want them?"

"Well, we're not being bombed and they've got to cross the killing zone."

"Okay," she said as if she didn't believe it.

Before Jefferson could speak, one of the enemy ships lifted straight up. The enemy began rushing through the opening, running across the open field, firing their lasers as they did.

From somewhere someone shouted, "Here they come."

Firing erupted from everywhere at them. The tracers lanced out. The enemy seemed unprepared for the sudden assault from the old-fashioned weapons. Their attack wavered, sputtered to a halt, and then they retreated. They never got closer than a couple hundred yards.

Through the whole thing, Jefferson stood near the entrance to the command bunker, ready to dive inside to direct the fighting if he needed to. But the crash from the rifles, and the pounding of the heavy machine guns was enough to turn the enemy. And with the pulse lasers firing at the ships, the enemy had no choice but to retreat.

As they turned, the soldiers began to cheer. A few of them raced from their bunkers, climbing up on top to harass the enemy as he ran.

Torrence looked at Jefferson and said, "That was much too easy."

"I know. I wonder if they weren't just testing our defenses so they could counter them."

"Pretty primitive way of doing that," she said.

Jefferson shrugged. "If you never had to fight because you held all the technological advantages, maybe you'd be fighting this war the same way. Learning as you go along."

"You'd think they'd be able to think it through."

"If you never had to do it, how would you fight?" Jefferson thought about that himself. It explained the lack of coordinated bombing, the lack of fire-and-maneuver tactics, and the lack of diversionary attacks. The enemy rushed at one side of his perimeter, trying to overrun it with sheer force. Not the best way to reduce an enemy position. Of course, he didn't mind because it just allowed him to chop up their forces.

The enemy's heavy lasers began to fire then. Bursts of light shot over them. Beams hit the bunkers and were absorbed. Jefferson's own lasers fired back to bleed off the excess of energy.

Jefferson slipped to one knee and watched what would have been called a counter-battery duel on old Earth. The infantry, dug in well, had no worry as the two sides used heavy weapons to fight.

Torrence yelled unnecessarily. "That'll tie them down for a while."

"Yeah." Jefferson turned and jerked on the handle of the blast door. "You keep watch. I'm going to see what happened to Clemens and the fleet."

"Yes, sir."

Jefferson ran down into the bunker. The technicians had taken cover under the tables and in the corners. The flatscreen was blank and two of the radios were filled with static.

"What the hell?"

The NCOIC, Cooke, climbed sheepishly to his feet. "Nothing coming in," he said.

"Damn it. We got people on the line fighting. The least you can do is man the radios."

"We could hear everything."

Jefferson pointed at the flatscreen. "What the hell is going on there?"

"Lost the signal from Clemens. He's moved out of range or is shielded by the planet. Davies should be able to see him if the problem is line of sight." Cooke didn't move toward the radios or the flatscreen. He stood his ground.

Jefferson wanted to scream at the man but knew it would do no good. He moved closer to the radios. "Are you in contact with Colonel Davies?"

"No, sir. We haven't been able to regain contact. The problem is at her end. We're transmitting."

"Okay." Jefferson looked at the people disgustedly. He shook his head and said, "Carry on. Oh, if you hear from Clemens, you get word to me."

"Yes, sir." The NCOIC moved toward the radio console and sat down. He studied the dials with an intensity that he hadn't felt since he'd first studied electronics.

Jefferson left the bunker and found Torrence kneeling near the blast door. She held her laser rifle in one hand. She hadn't traded it in on one of the older weapons.

"They're still not coming," said Torrence. "Keep firing at our heavy weapons but so far, no one's done any damage."

"Sappers," said Jefferson. "That's their problem. They don't have sappers to take out the heavy weapons or the reinforced bunkers.

He remembered a rain-pounded plain with a pillbox hammering in the night. His weapons, the bazookas and the machine guns, had been unable to destroy it. The slanted sides made it difficult to score a direct him. The rounds bounced off it. Mason had taken the satchel charges out, crawling through the night and the rain so that he could destroy it the old-fashioned way. Jefferson had gotten the credit, but Mason had done the work. Mason had used his knowledge of sappers to destroy the enemy pillbox.

"I guess they don't know about sappers. Of course, we're not using sappers either," said Torrence.

"We don't need to. We're in a defensive posture."

"Yes, sir."

At that moment, the enemy came on again. They rushed from a dozen positions, heading across the open killing field, their feet stirring up clouds of ash. They came on, screaming, firing their weapons, sounding as if they'd just gotten advice from Jeb Stuart's cavalry. Their voices were high, wailing like children.

The pulse lasers continued to fire, but the crews lowered the barrels, aiming at the oncoming enemy. The beams slammed into an energy net over the attackers. The lasers couldn't penetrate the screen.

But the men and women in the bunkers used their old rifles, pouring out a devastating fire. The slugs, the tracers, flashed out, hit the ground and bounced. Or smashed into the enemy, knocking them down.

"*Yeah!*" yelled Jefferson. "Give it to them!"

But this time the enemy didn't waver. They came on, passing the point they'd stopped at before. They didn't slow. They ran forward, heads bowed like men fighting a driving rain and high winds. They ran forward, firing from the hips, their laser beams striking the bunkers and being absorbed by them.

The noise rose until it was a continuous roar, overwhelming the individual sounds. Torrence, standing next to Jefferson, shouted something but he couldn't hear it. Too much noise from the firing and the screaming and the concussions of the grenades and mortars that had joined the battle.

Torrence fired her laser once. The beam struck the shield and was gone. The enemy seemed not to see it. Jefferson drew his pistol and fired once. The bullet hit an enemy soldier, knocking him to his rear. He sat there, a hand over the hole in his chest, surprised that he'd been hit.

And then they were at the edge of the bunker line. They were scrambling to climb it, to get on top of the bunkers, out of the line of fire.

Jefferson stood flatfooted, facing the enemy. He raised his pistol in both hands and fired at the mass climbing the bunkers. He saw two of the enemy fall and then his weapon was empty. He touched the button and watched the magazine fall from the butt of the weapon. He grabbed at his belt, freed a second magazine and slammed it home.

Now his soldiers were beginning to abandon their bunkers. They could no longer see the enemy and had to leave their protection to continue to fight.

Both Jefferson and Torrence ran forward, toward the line. A few of the enemy broke through and ran at them. Torrence went to one knee, firing her laser. The beam caught an enemy in the eye, exploding it. He shrieked and fell, both skinny hands over his face.

Jefferson stood next to Torrence, firing at the enemy. More of them were falling as the rounds found them. Their blood, as red as humans', splashed.

More of the humans were mixing with the enemy. Fighting was now hand to hand, but the humans had superior strength. They were lifting the enemy up and throwing them bodily back out of the perimeter. They were kicking them and smashing them. Enemy soldiers tried to fight back but didn't understand.

Jefferson and Torrence moved forward, toward one of the bunkers. As they approached, an enemy jumped at Jefferson. He turned and pushed, shoving the enemy to the ground. Before it could move, he shot it.

Slowly the humans were pushing the enemy off the bunkers. Jefferson climbed to the top of one, standing shoulder to shoulder with his soldiers. They fought, hitting, kicking and shooting the enemy.

Jefferson turned, saw one of his soldiers fall, blood boiling from a huge hole in her chest. Jefferson grabbed an enemy soldier by the back of the neck and lifted him high overhead. He slammed the enemy into the edge of the bunker, and even over the din of battle thought he heard the bones break. The enemy spasmed, kicked, and then was still.

Now the enemy was beginning to retreat, but they didn't understand how to do that either. They turned without orders and fled, leaving themselves open to the firing of the men and women who still manned the bunkers. The hammering of the weapons filled the air as more of the enemy died.

As they disengaged, the humans began to drop off the bunkers and seek cover behind them or to return to the interiors. The enemy lasers that had fallen silent as the enemy gained a foothold, began to fire again. But there were no longer any human targets. Those who still lived had taken cover.

Jefferson was sitting behind a bunker, his back to it, working to reload his pistol. Torrence ran toward him and knelt next to him. Neither could see the expression of the other. The hoods were still in place.

"Close," she said, breathing hard. "Very close."

"But we pushed them out again."

"Thanks to the troops."

"Yeah," said Jefferson. He finished reloading and looked up into the sky. "Where the hell is Clemens?"

"That's the question, isn't it?" she said.

"Yeah," he agreed. "That *is* the question."

17

FLAGSHIP OF THE TENTH INTERPLANETARY INFANTRY REGIMENT

CLEMENS DIDN'T LIKE running. It made him feel as if he was leaving friends behind to fight a battle that he was afraid to fight. But sometimes there was nothing that could be done. Orders were issued and had to be obeyed. And sometimes it was necessary to sacrifice lives for the greater good. Philosophers had argued the question for centuries, and he wasn't going to find the perfect solution while fighting a battle.

"Distance increasing," said one of his officers.

Clemens nodded but didn't speak. Instead, he kept his eyes on the flatscreen, watching the enemy formation. He'd inflicted damage. That was obvious.

"Location of our support ships?" asked Clemens.

"They're about ten thousand klicks from us, heading out of the system."

Clemens turned back toward the flatscreen. The enemy fleet had stopped its pursuit. They were drawing together, fifteen ships that were now between him and the planet where he'd left the infantry.

"Helm, let's slow to half speed. Communications, get me a damage report from the rest of the fleet."

"Helm, aye."

Clemens stood up and walked around the back of his chair. He leaned forward, his arms on the high back. Still he studied the screen, thinking that there had to be something that he had missed.

"Targeting, give me the status of the weapons systems."

"Targeting, aye. We've got about half the missiles left, eighty percent on torpedoes, and seventy percent on the sonic mines. Lasers and beams are fully charged. Shields are all operational and ready."

"Thank you." He looked at his staff on the bridge. "Any significant damage?"

"No, sir," said the executive officer.

Clemens rubbed his chin carefully. He stared at the flat-screen and tried to figure out why the enemy had broken the pursuit. He'd inflicted damage, but he'd taken it as well. He'd seen Dillard and her ships destroyed. He'd seen other vessels take hits. If the enemy continued the pursuit, there wouldn't be much Clemens could do.

"Helm, let's reverse course again. We're going back in."

"Aye, sir."

"Communications, get on the horn and alert the rest of the warships. Tell Morrow that he is still to maneuver for the safety of his ships."

"Aye, sir."

"Where's Boyson?"

"Boyson is trying to return to the fleet," said the plot officer.

"Helm, I want to approach close enough to open fire on the enemy fleet." He kept his eyes on the flatscreen and then realized that some of the enemy ships were missing. "Targeting?"

"Targeting, aye."

"The enemy fleet has fragmented. Do you have all his surviving vessels accounted for?"

"Targeting, wait one." There was nearly a full minute of silence, and then McCullough's voice came back, excited. "We have them all plotted. There are five in close proximity, coming from the right flank."

"Fire!" said Clemens. "You are cleared to open fire on them."

"Targeting, aye."

"Put them on the screen," he said.

The scene changed and he saw the five ships coming up, out of the glare of the system's star. Missiles from his own ship and that of two other captains appeared, diving at the enemy. The tiny rocket motors were nearly impossible to see against the brightness.

The enemy ships maneuvered as one, looking like old fighters in a close formation. They turned, pulling away, exposing the undersides. Beams, bright red light, stabbed out, reaching for the missiles. One by one, they exploded, disappearing from the flatscreen.

"Targeting," said Clemens.

This time no one replied. They fired again, more missiles, but this time they were accompanied by torpedoes and the lasers. The shields of the enemy began to glow, a dull green that was nearly invisible against the blackness of space.

"They're firing at us, Captain," called a voice.

Clemens had seen the rippling of light along the side of one of the enemy's ships. Missiles launched at him.

"Targeting?"

"We've got them, Captain."

Clemens saw the first of the enemy weapons vanish in a flash of brightness. He straightened up, becoming bored with the situation. He was gaining nothing. The enemy was still there. Still fighting.

One of the torpedoes punched through the enemy's defenses. It hit the front of an enemy ship and detonated. The ship dipped once and fire flared on the nose for an instant and then went out. The ship stabilized and held its position in the enemy formation.

Now other weapons were smashing through the enemy defenses. His beams reached out, destroying some of them. The explosions flashed like fireflies on a summer evening. It looked almost delicate, festive.

But the enemy retaliated, firing everything at them. A wave of enemy missiles and torpedoes coming straight at them. Clemens didn't move. Instead he ordered, "Helm, reverse. Full speed."

"Helm, aye."

Clemens waited for some feeling but it didn't come. They hung in space for a moment. "Helm," said Clemens.

"Helm, aye."

Then, suddenly, the ship reversed itself. Clemens felt his knees begin to buckle. He reached out and held on. The enemy missiles were bigger now, closer.

But Targeting was beginning to hit the incoming missiles. One by one they vanished.

"Communications, give me the rest of the enemy fleet."

The scene changed and Clemens saw the enemy had begun to withdraw. It was as if they were covering their retreat. And then he saw what they were doing. A few ships to hold him in place while the rest headed for the planet.

"Helm! Plot a course to the planet."

"Helm, aye."

"Targeting," said Clemens. "You're going to have to hit the main enemy fleet."

"Targeting, aye."

"Captain, they're turning to meet us," said the exec. "All of them."

Clemens understood exactly what that meant. He and the remnants of his fleet couldn't withstand a full attack by the enemy. There were too many of them.

"Helm, hold steady."

"Helm, aye."

"Targeting, spread of sonic mines. Missiles and torpedoes to follow."

"Targeting, aye."

Clemens was trying to put a spread of debris in the way of the enemy. It would slow them for a few moments. They would have to detour around it. That would delay them a couple of minutes but that could make all the difference.

Now Clemens and his fleet were speeding away from the battle again but this time the enemy fleet, the remaining ships, were following. It looked as if their plan was to destroy the human fleet once and for all.

Clemens moved around and sat down in his chair. The flatscreen showed the enemy fleet, the planets of the system, and the debris that the battle had created. The enemy was maneuvering, but he wasn't firing. Pursuit was the game at the moment.

"They're thirty seconds from the sonic mines," said a quiet voice.

Clemens didn't think they'd fall for that trick again. They had to know they were out there. Then, almost as if to prove it, the beams of the lead enemy ships fired, the targets were the mines. One by one they detonated. Flashes of brightness that burned out quickly. In a matter of moments, the enemy had burned a way through the minefield.

"Coming on again. They're accelerating."

"Targeting," said Clemens. "It's up to you."

"Targeting, aye."

Again the screen filled with missiles and lasers. Beams flashed and vanished. The missiles corkscrewed toward the enemy ships, but lasers from the enemy reached out and destroyed them.

"Bridge, we've depleted our store of missiles."

"Fire the torpedoes," said Clemens. He realized that firing all the torpedoes would leave them with only the defensive capabilities, but the problem was the soldiers on the ground. Clemens didn't want the enemy to be able to attack them from space.

"Targeting, aye."

Around him, the rest of the ships fired their weapons. Missiles and torpedoes. Space was filled with the pinpoints of light that marked the firing of the rocket engines. Lasers and particle beams punched out, glowing brightly. Space was crisscrossed with a glowing net of light in bright greens and reds and yellows. If it hadn't been for the deadly nature of the battle, Clemens would have marveled at the beauty of the displays.

To the left another of his ships was hit. The center of it began to glow brightly. The ends broke off, tumbling away. The center exploded.

"We've lost the *Topaz*," said the communications officer.

"Weapons status," said Clemens.

"We've zero missiles and ten percent of the torpedoes. Lasers and beams are fully charged."

"Fire a spread of the last torpedoes and throw out the remainder of the sonic mines."

"Targeting, aye."

Clemens waited for a moment and then said, "Helm, let's reverse again. Full speed at the enemy fleet."

"Helm, aye."

"Targeting, stand by," said Clemens.

"Targeting, aye."

Clemens watched as the range between the two fleets shortened quickly. They hadn't expected Clemens, who'd been running, to suddenly turn. They weren't prepared for it.

"All lasers, fire," ordered Clemens.

The beams flashed, playing across the closest of the enemy vessels. The ships disappeared in a sudden explosion. But the rest of the enemy fleet retaliated.

"Shields collapsing."

"Helm, reverse again. Let's get the hell out of here. *Now!*"

"Helm, aye."

"Captain, the *Georgia* has just vanished."

"Understood." Clemens didn't look at the communications officer. He kept his attention focused on the screen. The gap between him and the enemy was widening, but now they all came on. They weren't breaking the pursuit as they'd done before.

"Okay," Clemens said to himself. "Jefferson, I've done all I can for you."

"Captain?" said the exec.

"Nothing. Let's keep accelerating."

"Aye, sir."

"What's the status of the supply ships?"

"They're continuing to accelerate toward the Earth," said the plot officer. "They're now out of sensor range. Radio contact to them is now more than an hour."

"They're safe then," said Clemens.

"For the moment."

Clemens said, "Give me a shortened view on the flat-screen."

The scene there changed, showing the remnants of his fleet. Only three of the warships survived, though there might be people in the some of the wreckage. They'd have to check that closely, if they ever got the chance.

"Enemy coming at us rapidly. Firing all his weapons. Full spread of missiles."

"Targeting, take them out."

"Targeting, aye." The voice wasn't as calm as it had been. The strain of the battle was beginning to tell.

"I don't think they're going to get them all, Captain," said the exec.

"Close all the airtight doors and prepare to take a hit," said Clemens. He watched the screen as the first of the missiles flared into nothing. But there were more coming, beginning to evade in a complicated dance. The lasers flashed by them, sometimes brushing them, but unable to stay on them long enough to destroy them.

"Helm, let's evade."

"Helm, aye."

Clemens grabbed the arms of his chair, sure that they were going to take a deadly hit. Helplessness washed over him as he watched the missiles come closer. He didn't think his ship would live much longer.

18

ON THE PLANET'S SURFACE

JEFFERSON COULDN'T RESIST it. Leaning close to Torrence, he said, "They'll be back."

Torrence looked at the wreckage and the bodies scattered in the perimeter and said, "And I don't think we'll hold them this time."

Jefferson didn't want to confirm her opinion, but he thought the same thing. The enemy had pushed just hard enough to get over the perimeter and into the camp. But he hadn't been ready for that success. Having done it once, he would do it again, and this time there would be no reprieve.

Holstering his pistol, Jefferson got to his feet, but remained crouched, as if ready to spring at the enemy. "I'm going to the command bunker and see if we can raise Davies."

"They're all dead," said Torrence, her voice low, solemn.

"Of course," said Jefferson, "but we've got to try, just in case."

Jefferson leaped up and ran toward the blast door, hurtling the bodies of those killed. Medics moved among the wounded, trying to save lives. And four soldiers checked the enemy, killing the wounded because there was no way to treat them. Humans didn't have a clue about the bodies of the aliens, didn't understand their internal structures, and could do nothing to help them. The only course was to kill them so they wouldn't cause trouble during the next assault.

Jefferson reached the command bunker just as the enemy began the push. Lasers ripped the air. Beams danced across the bunker just above Jefferson's head and someone shouted in a panicky voice, *"Here they come again!"*

Dropping to his knees, Jefferson turned as the mass of alien soldiers poured from behind the protection of their makeshift fort and rushed across the open killing zone. The heavy weapons began to fire, and as the enemy got closer, the smaller rifles joined in.

But this time the enemy came on with the determination of an elemental force. There would be no stopping them. They would roll over Jefferson's tiny command in a matter of minutes, and there didn't seem to be a thing he could do to stop them.

Corporal Thomas Forest was in a corner bunker, leaning into the firing port, his rifle barrel inches from it. He was off to the side where he had the most protection. Two others were in there with him and none of them talked. The body of the fourth lay on the floor.

Forest emptied his weapon into the oncoming mass and then slipped to one knee. He jerked the empty magazine from his weapon and slammed in a new one. As he stood up, the side of the firing port erupted, blowing in. Splinters from the plastic embedded themselves in the mesh of his hood and shoulders.

"Christ!" he said, falling back.

"You hit?"

"No. No, I'm fine. Just a little close."

"They're almost here. Come on."

Forest climbed to his feet and leaned against the side of the bunker. He aimed and fired, first on single shot and then on full auto because the enemy was getting too close, and it seemed that nothing would stop them.

The interior of the bunker was heating rapidly. The odor of gunpowder filled it, making it hard to breathe. The acrid smoke stung the eyes, making it difficult to see.

"*Jesus!*" yelled one of the others. "How many of the fuckers are there?"

"I'm out of ammo," said another. He dropped to the floor and pawed at the body of the dead man. He pulled the ammo pouches free and took out the magazines.

"We're all getting low."

"What happens when we run out of ammo?"

"The fleet will be back," said Forest. "We've got to survive until the fleet gets here."

The enemy was much closer. Forest could see the faces of them. Gray faces with big, dark eyes. They held pistols or rifles in their skinny, three-fingered hands. Beams raked the bunkerline near them. Some pierced the firing port, striking the rear of the bunker but did no damage.

Forest twisted around, aiming at the enemy. He fired a short burst and saw two of the enemy fall. He emptied his weapon and said, "Reloading."

Susan Arnheeter sat in the seat behind the pulse laser. She bent forward, her eyes pressed against the sight. The computer moved the weapon, firing it at the closest of the enemy soldiers. Arnheeter was to make sure that it didn't make a mistake.

Sitting there, she was protected by a shield that absorbed the enemy's beams. She watched as the mass of alien soldiers came at her, the beams of her weapon diverted or absorbed by the enemy shield that protected them.

Firing from the enemy's heavy weapons began suddenly. The beams hit the bunker, the weapon and the shields but did no damage. It whirled her around as it began to target the enemy weapons. She held onto to the firing handles and felt the seatbelt tug at her belly and the straps cut into her shoulders.

The laser fired again and again, but now the beams passed over the enemy soldiers, striking the heavy weapons supporting them. She could barely make it out in the weapon's sight. A large, gray mass that flared as it tried to eliminate her weapon.

Next to her, one of the technicians was hit by the beam. His uniform absorbed most of the charge, but there was too much energy. He fell, screaming, as the beam cooked him from the inside out. He rolled over twice, tried to stand, and then fell, dying.

Arnheeter ignored him. She watched the numbers in the eyepiece and then squeezed the triggers she held, hoping to destroy the enemy's weapon.

The sensors registered the hits she was scoring. They were red flashes overlaid on the sight picture of the target. But she could see no damage being done. Their weapons were absorbing the punishment just as her own was.

Sarah Williams had abandoned the bunker, feeling too confined by it. She didn't like the odor or the heat in it, or having to listen to the breathing of the others. She wanted to concentrate on the battle and the noise and heat and odor was too distracting.

She lay behind the bunker, her body protected by it. She was peeking around the corner, her weapon aimed at the oncoming enemy. Training had taught her to fire at the closest enemy first because he was the most dangerous. But she had yet to fire. She wanted every shot to count and waited until the mass of the enemy was closer, jammed together so that even if she missed what she aimed at, the round would hit something.

The front ranks of the enemy attack were chopped to ribbons by the firing from the bunkers. They fell and tripped those behind them.

Williams finally fired on full auto, jerking the barrel back and forth like a fire fighter trying to kill the flames. Her tracers slammed into the leading rank of enemy, knocking them down. She held the trigger, burning through the whole magazine.

When her weapon was empty, she pulled back slightly and worked to reload it. Now she was aware of the noise around her. The screaming voices, the continuous roar of the weapons, and the electrical charge of the air. The hair on her body was standing upright, tickling her. It was a strange sensation. She was in a life-and-death fight, yet she was being tickled by her own body. It was more distracting than when she had been in the bunker.

The enemy came on, hundreds of them, all firing their

lasers, some of them brushing by her. She heard the quick hiss as a beam touched her shoulder and slid away. Her uniform bled the power off.

She rolled behind the bunker, reloaded and then peeked around again. The enemy was closer, running for her. She aimed and fired, this time in short bursts. She didn't want to burn out the barrel of her weapon.

There were others with her now. Men and women who had abandoned their bunkers again, and who were ready to meet the enemy head on. Firing from the grays increased into a long drawn out explosion that sounded like the buzzing of a hundred thousand angry wasps.

Williams emptied her weapon into the mass of alien soldiers. She saw blood burst on the chest of one and saw the head of another explode in a crimson cloud. They were falling and dying like soldiers on old Earth who had believed that dying in battle was a direct route to Heaven. They didn't care what was done to them. Their objective was to overrun the camp, and they weren't going to be turned back.

The men and women around her braced to meet the threat. They continued to shoot as the enemy beams touched them and were absorbed by the suits. At the moment, it looked as if the attack would fail.

Bruce Platt crouched in his bunker on the far end of the perimeter. Behind him he could hear the firing of the rest of the regiment. He, along with the rest of his company, was stuck facing the wrong way when the enemy attacked. Like the rest of the company, he'd wanted to abandon his position and jump into the fight. But they were guarding against a surprise attack from that quarter. They couldn't leave.

Platt moved to the rear of the bunker, stepped up and peered out. He could hear the firing and smell the battle. The shouts and screams cut through, and he wanted to join it, but the sergeant wouldn't let him.

"A dozen men can guard," said Platt.

"And a company can defend," said the sergeant. "Our job is to stay right here."

"Half the people," said Platt. "They may need the help."

The sergeant stood at the firing spot, staring out at the open ground. He glanced back over his shoulder at Platt. The sergeant knew what was happening outside and behind them.

"If they need help," he said, "they'll ask for it. Professionalism, Private Platt. That's the key to a winning army. And we *are* professionals. Sometimes what we have to do we find distasteful."

"But . . ."

"You get ready for the attack, Private," said the sergeant. "You wait right there and watch. You see an enemy soldier, you are cleared to fire."

"Yes, sergeant."

Corporal Cindy Hudson was in the center bunker which seemed to be the focus of the enemy attack. The two men and two women in there with her took turns at the firing port, two of them shooting with the other two reloading as the fifth looked out the rear of the bunker to make sure no one got behind them.

"Reloading," announced Hudson as she dropped back, away from the firing port.

She crouched and reached out to the ammo belts that were scattered on the floor among the empty brass, the discarded paper and the ripped-up boxes. She dropped the empty magazine into the trash and slammed another home.

She looked up and saw one of the women take a round in the head. Or a laser beam. She wasn't sure. She just heard the woman grunt in surprise. She dropped her rifle, turned and fell flat on her face.

Hudson reached over, tried to find a pulse and then ripped the woman's hood from her face. There was a neat, bloodless third eye in her forehead where the mesh of the uniform had failed to stop a laser. Her eyes were open but were bulged slightly, as if she'd been hit in the back of the head with a baseball bat.

"Karen's dead," she announced.

One of the men looked down at the body. "Shit," he said.

"Reloading," said the other. He dropped away from the firing port.

Hudson took his position, stunned to see how much closer the enemy was. There were covering the ground a little faster than she cared for.

The other man had taken a step forward so that the barrel of his rifle stuck out of the firing port. He fired a short burst, aimed again and fired again. The brass bounced off the plastic walls of the bunker, falling to the floor.

Hudson hesitated, looked, and then fired. Two of the enemy fell. Then a third and a fourth. She stepped back, ducked, and then popped up again.

"They're about to overrun us!" yelled the man. *"Kill them now."*

"Grenades," said Hudson.

The woman who'd been watching the rear turned and moved toward the firing port. She lifted her weapon which looked like a giant shotgun. She pulled the trigger and the first of the grenades fired. She let the huge cylinder rotate, the grenades firing one right after another.

But that didn't slow the enemy attack. They came on, ignoring everything around them. They reached the perimeter, hesitated momentarily and then crossed it.

"Okay," said Hudson. "Let's get the hell out of here." She pushed her way to the rear. At the door, she stopped, looking out. There were soldiers in the compound, fighting to keep the enemy from gaining a foothold.

There were no enemy soldiers visible. Hudson poked her head up and looked around. There was a line of soldiers lying on the ground, facing the enemy, firing at them. Two medics ran forward, grabbed a wounded soldier and dragged her to the rear. Another bent over a man lying on the ground. Laser beams flashed over their heads but they ignored them.

Hudson pulled herself out, stood and turned. She leveled her weapon but didn't fire it. Now she could see the whole panorama of the assault. Not just the few attacking her bunker, but all of them rushing forward. Thousands of them, supported by heavy weapons, came at the regiment. Hudson felt her stomach turn over as she realized the size of the attack and the slim possibility of turning it.

She stepped to the right and fired once, but didn't think it would do any good. Too many of the enemy and not enough of the regiment.

She emptied her weapon, stripped the magazine from it, but before she could reload, she was hit by an energy beam. She felt her uniform begin to heat. She dived to the right, behind the bunker, but the heat didn't go away, and the powerpack began to beep, signaling an overload. She dropped her weapon and struggled to pull the powerpack free. Just as she succeeded, it exploded. The last thing she saw was a flash of bright light and the last thing she felt was an incredible burst of pain.

19

ON THE PLANET'S SURFACE

JEFFERSON REMAINED CLOSE to the command bunker where he could see everything that was happening around him. Torrence had run off to the line and was directing the firing, trying to stop the tide of enemy soldiers. Jefferson wasn't sure they could do it. He wasn't sure the regiment would last another hour.

He crouched, his pistol in hand, and watched as the enemy hit the bunkerline and rolled over it. He watched his soldiers pour from the bunkers to counterattack but it didn't look good. They were swallowed by the tide of the enemy.

An NCO appeared at his side and Jefferson said, "You'd better get the rest of the regiment together. Leave one man in four on the opposite side, but we've got to throw everyone into this."

"Yes, sir."

Jefferson opened the blast door and shouted down. "Get Clemens and tell him that we're losing it. I want one man to remain behind. The rest of you up here."

He whirled without waiting for an answer. He ran forward a dozen steps and then aimed his pistol at the swarming enemy soldiers. He fired at them, emptying it into their ranks. Then he turned and retreated. He just didn't know what in the hell he was going to do.

Torrence ran toward the right end of the line and dived into the bunker that housed one of the pulse lasers. There were two soldiers lying dead on the floor and another, a wounded woman, sitting back against the wall, a hand pressed to her bleeding shoulder.

Arnheeter still sat in her seat, her eye pressed to the sight, as she searched for targets. The weapon was whirling around, aiming itself at the enemy.

The interior of the bunker was hot. That was from the incoming enemy energy beams, the working of the electrical systems and the firing of the old weapons.

Torrence moved toward the view port. In the distance, over the onrushing enemy mass, she saw the heavy weapons firing in return. Red and green beams, barely visible in the sunlight, flashed toward them, hit the absorbing mass of wire mesh and were gone.

"Not getting anywhere," yelled Arnheeter. "Just firing and firing but not getting anywhere."

Torrence knew that was the complaint of artillery officers during counter-battery duels. They could see no results, but they couldn't stop firing because that gave the advantage to the enemy.

"You're doing fine," said Torrence.

Arnheeter didn't answer as the weapon rotated suddenly, fired, and rotated again.

Torrence slipped to the rear, to the wounded woman and looked into her eyes. She reached out and pulled the hood from the woman's head. Her skin was waxy looking, the sweat beaded on it, and Torrence knew the woman was dying.

Stepping to the doorway, she looked out and yelled, "Medic!" But there was no response to it. The medics were all busy trying to save the wounded they had already found.

Torrence ducked back and crouched. She patted the woman on the thigh and said, "You'll be all right. Medic's on the way."

The woman tried to smile, but blood rushed from her mouth,

covering her chin and splashing down the front of her uniform. She slumped to the right as she died.

Turning, Torrence yelled at Arnheeter, "Stay with it as long as you can."

But then the front of the bunker seemed to superheat, melt, and then explode inward. Torrence was knocked from her feet and slammed against the rear of the bunker.

She looked up to see the front of the pulse laser disintegrate. Arnheeter tried to scramble from the seat and was caught by a high-energy beam. It baked her as quickly as a microwave oven. She screamed for an instant and then pitched forward, the stench of roasted meat filling the bunker.

Torrence, now lying across the legs of the dead woman, tried to push herself up but couldn't find the strength. She collapsed for the moment, unable to even think about her next move.

The enemy had overrun part of the line. Forest had enemy soldiers in front of him and behind him now. He was crouched in the doorway of the bunker, protecting it from the enemy who were leaping to the top of the bunker and dropping down in the rear of it.

He fired into a crowd of enemy soldiers. They fled, scattering right and left. Forest shifted around, spotted another and shot again. This time he was successful. The enemy dropped to the ground and didn't move.

Behind him, inside the bunker, the firing was as heavy as ever. The hammering of the weapons, the pounding noise amplified by the plastic walls, the acrid stink of the gunpowder, gave him a blinding headache. He wanted to get out into the cooler, quieter air outside.

Something hit the bunker near his head, ripping away a portion of the plastic. Forest jumped back and slid down into the protection of the bunker.

"Shit. That was close," he said. But the others ignored him. They were fighting for their lives.

He stepped back and glanced out. A hundred of the enemy were behind him, attacking the other bunkers, attacking the soldiers in the open, and pushing toward the command bunker.

Forest fired at the enemy. One of them dropped, rolling

away. He shot again, missed and fired a third time. Now some of the enemy turned toward him, returning fire. Chunks of the plastic broke off. Parts of it melted. They enemy began to scatter, launching an attack on the bunker.

Forest fell back slightly and fired out, trying to keep the enemy away from him. One of them ran forward with something in its tiny hand. Forest shot at it and missed. Suddenly, it dived to the ground and tossed the object. Forest stepped out, caught it and tossed it back. The device exploded, spraying shrapnel. The concussion caught him and threw him back. Bits of metal ripped into his uniform but didn't penetrate it.

He leaped up, shaking his head. His eyesight was blurry, making it difficult to see the enemy. He saw shapes but couldn't tell if they were friend or foe. He slipped back and shook his head.

But as he moved to the doorway a third time, a shape loomed over him. Forest didn't hesitate. He fired his rifle from the hip. Blood splattered him as the creature screamed in sudden pain.

It let go of something. Forest saw the shape fall, but in the clutter at the bottom of his bunker, he couldn't see it. "Grenade," he screamed.

The others turned and one fell to the floor. The grenade detonated in a blinking flash of bright light and a deafening roar that was reflected by the walls of the bunker. The concussion was held in place and focused, ripping at the men and women inside.

Forest knew he was falling but couldn't stop it. Suddenly everything was quiet and everything was bright and a peacefulness swept over him. All his troubles had suddenly ended. He dropped to the debris-covered floor, never realizing that he'd been killed.

Williams stood up to meet the onrushing enemy. She had been lying behind a bunker, picking off the enemy one by one as they rushed across the open ground. She was up on her knees, firing as fast as she could pull the trigger, and then switching to full auto as the enemy closed on her.

As they got closer, she realized that there would be no

turning them back. They were going to breach the perimeter and get inside it. There was nothing she could do about it except to keep firing, trying to kill those who were coming at her.

One of the aliens leaped atop the bunker and Williams fired once. The creature flipped back, disappearing as it fell.

Williams dropped to the ground and reloaded rapidly. When she popped up again and began shooting, she twisted around as she spotted targets. One shot and then on to the next, killing those closest first. She shot right, left, then right and right, and then whirled to fire into a cluster of enemy soldiers running past her.

She emptied her weapon again, but now there was no time to reload. The enemy was there, attacking her. She clubbed one with the butt of her rifle. It spun and fell. But there was another one there, moving in on Williams. She swung, hit it in the head and then fell back. As she did, one of the creatures fired at her.

Williams kicked out and swept the legs out from under the being. She heard the fragile bones snap. As the enemy fell, Williams kicked once more, killing it. Then she stumbled and fell.

Now she was down and the enemy sensed the kill. They swarmed at her, firing at her, trying to smash her with the butts of their weapons. Williams rolled to the right, up against the rear of the bunker. She swung her weapon and then tossed the rifle away, grabbing her pistol. She shot the closest of the enemy soldiers. It fell toward her, landing on her legs, pinning her to the ground. She kicked and then pulled a foot free. She shoved on the body, pushing it off her feet.

Another enemy came at her. She fired up and killed it. But there was another one and she missed with the first shot. The second killed it.

The enemy was up on top of the bunker looking down at her. Williams fired, missed and fired again. She hit that one, but it was replaced by another, shooting down at her. The beams missed her or were absorbed by her uniform.

But there were too many of them now. She emptied her pistol and struggled to get up. One of the creatures struck her, knocking her back. She rolled over to get her hands and feet under her. She leaped up and swung around, knocking an enemy soldier to the ground.

Another of the enemy fired, and this time the beam stabbed through the eyeholes of Williams's hood. The pain was tremendous. She screamed and rolled up against the bunker again. She tried to fight back but couldn't see the enemy. She was out of ammo and weapons and luck.

One of the enemy grabbed her hood and jerked it from her head. As it did that, its partner fired a laser at her face. Williams died in a blast of bright light.

Jefferson rallied the remainder of the regiment around him. It included the men and women from the opposite side of the perimeter and those who'd been forced from their bunkers. The enemy was swarming all over the perimeter, jumping into the bunkers and taking them as their own. The firing hadn't slowed.

Waving a hand, Jefferson yelled, "*Let's go!*"

They surged forward, wading into the fight, weapons firing. The first rank of the enemy went down in a matter of seconds. But the resolve of the others stiffened.

They pushed forward, fighting to retake the line. Jefferson fired slowly, deliberately, picking his targets. He watched two of the enemy die as he fought his way closer to the bunkerline.

Now there was nothing on his mind at all. No great strategies. He just wanted to push the enemy from the camp. When that was done, he could worry about the next hour.

Behind him there was a shattering explosion, and he was thrown to the ground along with everyone else. For a moment he thought he was too badly wounded to stand, but the pain drained away and he found that he could move.

He got up slowly. Everyone, both his regiment and the attacking enemy had been dazed by the explosion. Jefferson turned and saw a smoking ruin where the command bunker had been. There were bodies scattered around it, men and women killed in the explosion.

"Take them!" yelled Jefferson. He waved his people forward. He fired as fast as he could, knocking the enemy down.

They all ran forward to the bunkerline. Jefferson slammed into the enemy line, striking out, killing enemy soldiers. He was screaming at the top of his lungs, swinging right and left, killing the enemy.

The enemy fell back under the surging charge led by Jefferson. They jumped from the bunkers and ran across the open ground, some of them forgetting their weapons. Panic spread through them as they tried to get away from the screaming human soldiers.

Jefferson fired at the fleeing enemy and then whirled. He dropped to the rear of the bunker, leaning close against it. "Who's in there?" he called. Pass words and codes weren't important here. The enemy couldn't speak enough English to matter.

"Colonel?"

"Yeah."

"Coming up and out."

"Come ahead."

One man reached out and pulled himself up. He was a young man with a rip in his uniform and blood splattered on it. He grinned, his teeth barely visible because of the hood. "Platt," he said.

"Anyone else in there?"

"No, sir. They're dead."

Jefferson slipped to one knee. The firing was tapering as the enemy got out of range. The heavy weapons, fired from behind the enemy's ships, fell silent but the air was still electric from the beams.

Platt looked around at the destruction inside the camp, at the debris scattered on the ground, at the abandoned equipment and the bodies of the dead. Portions of the bunkerline were little more than smoking ruins, the material used to build them spread out behind them. He saw the gaping wound that had been the command bunker and the ruins of the other structures. "Good God, it was close."

"Closer than you think," said Jefferson.

A sergeant appeared and asked, "Orders?"

"Organize the survivors into two battalions with the senior surviving officers in command."

"Yes, sir."

He looked back at the bunker. "We have any radio equipment left?"

"Yes, sir. Short-range stuff. Not much of it."

"Then I guess we're on our own."

"Yes, sir," said the sergeant.

"They going to attack again?" asked Platt.

Jefferson looked at the enemy formations and then at the remains of his camp. "They'd be stupid not to."

20

FLAGSHIP OF THE TENTH INTERPLANETARY INFANTRY REGIMENT

CLEMENS DIDN'T THINK he'd be able survive another hour. His fleet was in ruins, the majority of the combat vessels either gone or so heavily damaged that they were little more than traveling junkyards.

He sat on the bridge and listened to the groaning of his own dying ship. The screens had collapsed for a single, brief instant, but it had been enough time for the enemy to hit him with two missiles.

Now he, along with the crippled remnants of his fleet, were maneuvering away from the Eighty-two Eridani system. He was still between the enemy and his support vessels, and the enemy had not turned to return to the planet, but all that was merely a matter of time.

Clemens sat there, wanting to call on Targeting, but knew the weapons had all been used. The laser and particle beams were at half power because they'd had to divert power from them to hold the screens up. The sonic mines had been spread and the enemy was long past them.

"Communications," said Clemens.

"Communications, aye."

"Better dispatch a drone. Full reports and our last position.

Suggest there are survivors here and that they should make an effort to locate them."

There was a long hesitation and then, "Communications, aye."

"Helm, how are we doing?"

"Engine power is down and we have almost no ability to maneuver quickly. Enemy is beginning to close the gap and will be in effective range in twenty minutes."

"Captain, we've got another group of ships coming in from the distance. At the very limits of our range."

"How many ships?"

"Quite a few. I can't get an accurate count."

Clemens laughed once. It was the cross between a snort and a chuckle. "That's it then. They've got this system. Next stop will be Earth."

"Division," said the executive officer.

Clemens shook his head but said nothing. He couldn't tell them that the division was spread too thin and that with the elimination of Jefferson's light brigade and his fleet, the enemy would roll over the remainder of the division. They had wasted their assets by dividing them and deploying them so far apart.

"New fleet is beginning to accelerate," said the plot officer.

"Bridge, Targeting. Enemy fleet is beginning to slow down now."

"Bridge, aye," said Clemens as he rocked back and wondered why he was getting the reprieve. And then he thought that he understood it. They could deal with him at any time. He was no longer important. Now they had to destroy the force on the planet's surface.

"Helm," said Clemens. "Reverse again."

"You're going to attack?" asked the helmsman.

"You have your orders," said Clemens. "Targeting, let's stand by."

"Targeting, aye."

"Captain, there is nothing we can do for the people on the ground, and we still have the support fleet to protect."

Clemens nodded, understanding the argument completely. It made no sense to attack the enemy, knowing that they would have to fail. But sometimes that was the only thing you could do. Make a final, blazing statement. Let the enemy know that no matter how battered you are, if there is a single, impossible chance for victory, you'll take it. With that in the enemy's mind, he might be less inclined to attack.

But Clemens couldn't tell his crew that he was about to make the ultimate sacrifice because he had no right to make that choice for them all. Or maybe he did. As commander, he often made life-and-death decisions without consulting those who were to die.

Besides, they wouldn't live forever. No matter how careful they were, no matter how much attention they paid to personal health, hygiene and diet, something would eventually get them. What difference did a few years make? Especially if they could do nothing to protect the Earth.

"Targeting, can you get a solid lock on any of their vessels?"

"Targeting, aye. All weapons locked onto a single target."

"Stand by," said Clemens. "Communications, can you give me a better look at the new arrivals?"

"Communications, aye. On the screen now."

There was something about the new fleet that struck Clemens as odd. They didn't look as if they belonged to enemy's fleet.

"Close up?" asked Clemens.

"Full magnification now, Captain."

Clemens stood and walked across the bridge, leaning close to the flatscreen. He reached up and touched it and then looked at the assembled men and women on the bridge. With a grin spreading across his face, he said, "The newcomers are ours."

Jefferson stood with the new surviving members of his staff. Torrence, who had been wounded, had been carried to a point where she would be protected during the fighting. She and the other wounded would be safe unless Jefferson and the regiment lost the fight.

Jefferson studied the two men and single woman standing there. Courtney Norris, the supply officer who had demanded that she deploy with the regiment was dead. Killed when her bunker was overrun. Carter, the intelligence officer, died in the open, fighting until his weapon ran out of ammo and the enemy attacked him by the dozen. Peyton, the operations officer, died in the explosion of the command bunker. Jefferson was left with Winston, the personnel officer, Thompson, the assistant operations manager, and Scott, the executive officer of the First Battalion.

Winston was the first to speak. "I haven't been able to get a good count, but we've taken better than fifty percent casualties. We'll never withstand another attack."

Jefferson stared at him and then said, "It's the only choice we have." He looked into their faces and realized that each of them was scared. They'd watched as too many of their fellow soldiers were killed. They knew the enemy now held all the cards.

"I won the Galactic Silver Star," said Jefferson. For a moment he was going to confess the truth, that Mason had actually won it but that the army had given it to him. Instead, he heard himself saying, "I think that men and women win these things because there is no other choice. We have to be brave now because we are forced into a corner. We can either fight and die or we can run and die. It makes no difference, because in the end, we die."

He looked again at the young officers. "We can bullshit the troops, put on a brave face. It's much harder to succumb to cowardice when everyone else is brave."

"Why?" asked Thompson. "Just tell me why?"

"Because there is nothing else we can do. We have no more choices here."

"Escape and evasion," said Winston.

"To where?" asked Jefferson. "Nowhere to go. No lines of soldiers for protection. No safe haven anywhere for us to escape and evade to."

"Surrender?" asked Thompson.

"Will they take prisoners?" asked Jefferson. "And if they do, we'll end up as slaves. We've already seen how that works."

"Better than being dead," said Thompson.

"That we don't know," said Jefferson. He studied the officers with him for a moment. Tired, dirty people, the looks in their eyes like those of condemned men. They knew that in the next hour or so they were going to die. He knew that they all hoped for a reprieve, that the governor would call to stop the execution. Except there was no governor and there was no hope. The deck was stacked against them.

Finally, he said, "Okay. Let's get back on the line. They'll be coming again. Do the best you can and I'll . . . " He stopped talking, unsure of how to procede. They had run out of everything. Help would not come in time. There was no one to help.

Then, quietly, Jefferson said, "Do the best you can. That's all we can ask."

The staff officers turned toward him and came to attention. As if ordered to do it, they all saluted. Jefferson returned it and said nothing about it. In the field they didn't often salute, but with the regiment about to die, it didn't matter anymore.

As they headed toward the bunkerline, Jefferson walked toward the makeshift hospital. He found Torrence lying on the ground, a bandage around her shoulder and chest. Her hood had been removed, and he could see her pale, sweatsoaked face and hair.

Crouching next to her, he took her gloved hand. "How are you doing?"

She shook her head. "I'm okay. Should be on the line."

Jefferson glanced at the others around her. Men and women who had been wounded in the fighting. Lowering his voice, he said, "You will be soon enough."

"That bad?"

"Let's just say that they won't get the regimental colors. Those were left on the ship. I doubt that the enemy will be able to board it. The colors will be lost but not captured."

Tears welled in her eyes. "Damn it all anyway. Why'd they have to abandon us?"

"Nothing they could do," said Jefferson. "We're buying time so they can get ready to defend the Earth."

"Still . . . "

Again, he glanced at the others around her. "I . . . I just wanted to say good-bye. I don't think we'll withstand another assault."

She struggled to sit up. "Then I might as well join you on the line."

"No," said Jefferson. "I want you here. Maybe you can save some of the wounded. Maybe once the shooting is over, they'll take care of the wounded."

"I don't want to be captured," said Torrence. "I went that route once."

"Your job now is to save as many of the wounded as you can," he said.

"Yes, sir," she said. She looked up at him, almost spoke, and then didn't

Without a word from her, Jefferson said, "I know. It's the same for me." He squeezed her hand and then stood up. "See you later."

"Yes, sir."

He walked away, never looking back. He couldn't stand the sight of her lying there, nearly helpless. When the enemy eliminated the resistance, he didn't think they'd take the wounded captive. It was his belief that the regiment was dead. It was in the process of dying.

At the bunkerline, he dropped down into a hole and pushed his way past the debris that choked it. From the firing port, he could see out over the open field where the scattered bodies of the enemy dead lay. It was a scene that could have been played out in front of Roman legions, the Confederate or Union forces of the American Civil War or Marines landing on beaches in the Pacific. War had changed only in the places where it was fought. It still came down to the strength of the enemy. If he was stronger, then he won. If not, he lost.

Jefferson checked his weapons, making sure they were fully loaded. He arranged his grenades in front of him, and he put a laser pistol down near them. He was ready. It was up to the enemy to come at them. He would make them pay dearly, and he would, at least in his own eyes, have finally paid for the medal he'd won so long ago.

There was never any shout of warning. The enemy didn't blow bugles to announce the attack. They didn't try to prep the area with artillery. All they did was begin running across the open ground quietly, hoping to cross most of it before the firing began.

Forest, who had been sitting in his bunker, not watching for the enemy, just waiting for him, turned and looked out the firing port. He spotted the enemy coming at him and pushed his weapon out, aiming. He said nothing as he began to fire.

There was no one else with him in the bunker. The wounded had been carried away, and the dead were left where they fell. He fired at the oncoming enemy, letting his training take over. He was no longer thinking about it. Just aim and fire. Aim and fire. Aim and fire.

But with so many in the regiment dead, the enemy didn't have much trouble crossing the open ground. They came on rapidly, firing from the hip as the heavy weapons behind them opened up in support.

Forest emptied his weapon, ducked and reloaded. He popped up again, fired a single round and was hit full in the chest by one of the enemy's heavy lasers. The beam was absorbed for a moment and then burned through.

Forest didn't say a word. He didn't scream. He sat down hard and then fell to the side. He was dead as he hit the deck.

Platt, with two others, fired at the oncoming enemy, killing them as fast as they could. Platt didn't speak to the others. One of them was screaming at the top of his voice. Just screaming in a constant wail that didn't seem to stop so that he could breathe.

Platt emptied his weapon and yelled, "Reloading!"

Neither of them looked at him. They just kept firing, ducking to reload. Everyone was burning through the ammo as fast as he could fire it. They now believed that the only way they could survive was to throw out a wall of lead.

The man to the right took a hit, stopped screaming, and then fell back. Blood spurted from a hole in his chest. A crimson fountain that splashed the wall behind him and filled the bunker with the odor of hot copper and bowel.

"Terry?" yelled Platt, looking down at the bleeding body. "Terry?"

"He's dead, damnit. Shoot or we're going to join him."

And then the second man was hit. He staggered to the rear, looked at the stain spreading on the front of his uniform. He sat down and them slumped over, dead.

Platt could take it no longer. He scrambled from the bunker. As soon as he was out, he whirled and opened fire again. But the enemy had crossed most of the open ground and were beginning to squirm up and over the bunkerline. The fighting would quickly become hand to hand.

Platt was hit then. A single wound high on his shoulder. He fell back and landed hard. The wound wasn't fatal, but he knocked himself out when he fell.

The defense of the bunkerline collapsed in a matter of moments. The enemy overran it, screaming their hatred for the humans. They came on firing. Jefferson's soldiers were falling rapidly. Defense was nearly eliminated. The regiment was in its last moments.

He fell back with a knot of men and women, thinking that they might be able to save the wounded. Fight the enemy to a standstill so that the wounded would have a chance as the battle ended.

But there were too many of them coming too fast. He watched as Thompson died under an assault of a dozen alien soldiers. Scott lasted a moment longer but she too was killed. Winston fell wounded and didn't move.

Jefferson and a small group of soldiers stood in a small knot, fighting on. They stood in a square as the aliens came at them, shrieking their anger. Jefferson fired quickly, watching many of the aliens die.

From somewhere, a voice called, "Help me. Help me. Someone, please."

Jefferson turned and saw a lone soldier surrounded by the enemy. They were poking at him. They were dancing around him like savages who sensed the kill. But there was nothing Jefferson could do about it.

And then, suddenly, as if God was angry, came a loud roar from overhead. There was a gigantic crash in the distance. An explosion that ripped up the ground and tossed it up into the air. The concussion rolled over them, trying to knock them all from their feet. Heat, from the detonation, reached them a moment later.

"What the hell?"

There was a second and then a third explosion. Jefferson was shaken from his feet. He fell on his side, his arm under him. He heard rather than felt the bones snap.

He looked up beyond the bunkerline and saw a cloud of smoke and debris hanging over the enemy camp. And out of the bright blue of the sky came a flash of silver as a ship dived, dropping a bomb.

"My God," yelled someone. "It's one of ours!"

"Holy Mother of God!"

Jefferson couldn't believe it. He knew it was some kind of trick. A way for the enemy to save a few of his soldiers by diverting their attention. "*Kill them!*" shouted Jefferson. "Kill the enemy!"

But the complexion of the battle had changed suddenly. No longer was the regiment dying. It was sick, it was badly wounded, but suddenly it looked as if it might survive.

Jefferson felt a sudden burst of energy. He leaped to his feet. He was screaming, firing at the enemy, watching them fall. He took a step forward. No longer was it a holding action. No longer was he putting off his death. Now, suddenly, with the appearance of that ship, he was on the attack. His life would not end on that planet.

The firing was tapering as the enemy tried to get out. The fight no longer interested them. They saw the bombing begin and knew that something had happened in space. Now it was they who were in danger. They had to get out.

Firing from the enemy's heavy weapons was suddenly directed skyward. One of the ships lifted off suddenly, wobbled, and then flashed away to the south, staying low.

One of the surviving heavy weapons in Jefferson's regiment opened fire again. It was aimed at the fleeing enemy ship, but then the barrels were lowered and it raked the retreating soldiers.

More bombs fell and laser beams danced from the sky. One enemy ship vanished in a sudden flash of bright light as a laser touched it. The booming explosion shook the ground. Bits of the craft rained down on the perimeter. Small, hot bits of metal that couldn't be identified.

Jefferson, who'd managed to stand, was knocked from his feet again. He twisted as he fell and didn't injure his already broken arm.

The enemy soldiers were running across the open field, trying to get back to their ships before they were left behind. They forgot about the humans they had been trying to kill. They forgot about the battle they had been fighting. Now they only thought about reaching the safety of their ships. Reaching their ships and getting off the planet.

Jefferson rolled over and yelled, "Form a skirmish line. Form a skirmish line. Keep firing." The pain in his arm was making him sick. He couldn't stand or move. He watched as his soldiers did as ordered.

Others ran for the bunkerline. They threw themselves down and aimed at the enemy. They killed more of them as the bombs continued to fall. More of the enemy ships were smashed, disappearing in flashs of light.

Torrence appeared suddenly and knelt near Jefferson, who was now sitting, cradling his broken arm. She watched the enemy for a moment and then looked into Jefferson's eyes. She asked, "What in the hell happened?"

For a moment he didn't respond. For a moment, he wasn't sure what had happened and then suddenly, he knew. "We won," he said. "We really won."

"How?" she asked.

"I don't know, but we did. Battle's over now." He looked at her, the surprise showing bright in his eyes. "And we're still alive. Both of us."

The reality of the situation wouldn't sink in for a couple of hours.

EPILOGUE

FLAGSHIP OF THE TENTH INTERPLANETARY REGIMENT

SITTING IN THE remains of his cabin, looking at the computer that no longer worked, Jefferson was aware of the pain in his arm. The break had been bad, and by the time he got into surgery, after a couple of days, it was infected. They had rushed him through because the doctors were tired and there were still a hundred people requiring treatment.

But Jefferson didn't call the ship's doctor or the regimental surgeon to get something for the pain. He didn't want to bother anyone. He just wanted to sit in his cabin, stare at the broken computer and try to keep his mind blank.

There was a bong at the hatch. He glanced at it but the camera system was no longer working. The only way to find out who it was was to open the hatch. Jefferson decided that he didn't care enough to get up.

But the hatch opened and Torrence entered. She was wearing a new uniform. There was a bandage wrapped around her left hand and she was limping slightly.

She looked at Jefferson and asked, "You going to eat?"

"Nope."

"Why not?"

"Not hungry."

Torrence wanted to sit down but there was no place other than the cot. The plastic chair that had been in front of the desk was gone. To compromise, she leaned back against the bulkhead. "Just what in the hell is wrong with you?" she demanded.

"Wrong with me?"

"Yeah. You've been locked up here ever since we got off the planet's surface."

"So what?"

Torrence looked at him closely. She shook her head and then studied the deck. "I don't understand."

Jefferson felt the emotion that he'd kept bottled up in him bubble to the surface. Words that he thought he'd never say to another human were suddenly pouring from his lips.

"What's not to understand? I lost the regiment. Watched as it died on the planet's surface. Seventy-eight percent of the people dead."

"And the enemy is on the run," said Torrence.

"Not because we did anything," said Jefferson. "The results would have been the same if we'd never been there."

"Are you that shortsighted?" asked Torrence.

"I killed the regiment."

"The regiment still lives," said Torrence. "Just as the Seventh survived the Little Bighorn and the Twenty-fourth lived beyond Isandhlwana. It lives in the hearts of the survivors. Garvey has filed more than a dozen stories about the regiment and the heroes of it."

"Crap," said Jefferson.

"Fine," said Torrence. "Wollow in your self-pity."

"I destroyed the regiment."

"You did what you had to do. You did what needed to be done."

"I did what anyone could have done. Stood and fought and watched as the people died."

"Oh, forget it," said Torrence. She waved a hand at him. "Just forget it."

"I'll never forget it," said Jefferson. "Never."

"Any excuse to give up," said Torrence. "Pressure of command too much for you? Now you can just give up."

Jefferson snorted. "Nothing left to command anyway."

"Oh, Christ," snapped Torrence.

Jefferson sat quietly for a moment, letting his thoughts run wild. Davies had been wiped out. They'd found half a dozen people from that battle. Had it not been for her, his regiment would have been overrun faster. She'd been nominated for the Galactic Silver Star, but Jefferson didn't think she'd get it. The army still preferred living heros to dead ones.

But the commanding general, in a ceremony held on his flagship a day earlier, had made a speech and added a streamer to the divisional flag to remind others of the sacrifice. In that respect, Davies and her regiment still lived.

Of course, no one had made similar statements about his regiment. It hadn't been wiped out. There was no streamer for the divisional flag.

And then suddenly he understood it. Torrence was right. The regiment did still live. It lived in his heart and his memories and in those who had been on that planet. They could rebuild it. There would be whispered conversations about the battle and how they had been on the verge of extinction and had managed to hang on for just a moment.

Would Custer and his Seventh Cavalry have survived if the whole regiment had died at the Little Bighorn? Would people still talk about it if the regiment had ceased to exist?

He looked at Torrence and realized what she was trying to say. He'd done what had to be done. He and the regiment had been placed in an almost indefensible position, and they had held out. They had stopped the enemy long enough, and then the rest of the division had arrived to end the fight. There was no reason for him to feel that he'd failed.

Torrence, sitting quietly, saw the changes as they shifted around Jefferson. She could see him processing the information and fitting it in with the facts as they knew them.

Finally he said, "You mentioned lunch?"

"I mentioned something to eat."

"Okay. Let's go eat."

"And then?"

Jefferson shrugged. "And then we get back to work. Build the regiment again. That's what it's all about."

Torrence sat for a moment and nodded. "Yeah," she said. "That's what it's about."